"We think we heard a noise in the direction of the last room on the hallway," I said.

No one moved.

"We haven't got all day." Sam shouldered past us.

We stood in a tight cluster by the front door as he went down the hallway. We could hear him opening doors, turning lights on and off, and shutting doors again as he moved toward the end of the hall.

I found myself walking alone toward the archway, drawn to the hallway, holding my breath as I waited for Sam to reach that last room.

I heard him bump something as he fumbled for the light switch. As a patch of light spread into the end of the hall, Sam gave a gasping, guttural cry. He backed into the hall, turned, and staggered toward us, his face distorted by the shadows, and his eyes glittering.

"No!" he said. "There's—"

He suddenly reached out both arms to clutch at me, but his eyes rolled up, and he fell, dragging me with him

A DEADLY GAME OF MAGIC

JOAN LOWERY NIXON

HARCOURT, INC.

Orlando   Austin   New York   San Diego   Toronto   London

www.HarcourtBooks.com

First Harcourt paperback edition 2004

The Library of Congress has cataloged the
hardcover edition as follows:
Nixon, Joan Lowery.
A deadly game of magic/Joan Lowery Nixon.
p. cm.
Summary: Lisa and her three friends find themselves
unwilling players in a cat-and-mouse game with a murderous
magician whose identity and motivation baffle them.
[1. Mystery and detective stories.
2. Magic tricks—Fiction.]
I. Title.
PZ7.N65Daz 1983
[Fic]—dc19   83-8379
ISBN 0-15-205030-2 pb

Text set in Minister Book
Designed by Scott Piehl

G H F

Printed in the United States of America

To my sister,
Patricia Lowery Collins,
with love

A DEADLY GAME OF MAGIC

[ONE]

A SPRING RAIN slithered over the car windows in a blinding liquid sheet. It surged against the rhythmically creaking wipers that failed to sweep the heavy water from the windshield.

I leaned forward, gripping the dashboard, trying to peer through the downpour and the dark. "I can't see the road!" I said.

"It doesn't matter, Lisa. You're not driving. I am," Bo snapped.

"We should have taken the main highway." I knew I should keep quiet. He probably felt as tense as the rest of us did. But I didn't like Bo Baxter, and I knew he didn't like me.

"Shut up, Lisa!" Teena Wilson spoke up from the backseat.

Julian didn't say anything, and I didn't expect him to. Julian Hamilton IV was a loner who acted as though he weren't interested enough in anyone to carry on a conversation. Julian was tall and very slender—"slight," my grandma would have called him, "as though he needed some good home cooking"—so different from Bo, with his big, sun-browned body, the same color as his thick curly hair.

There we were, the four of us, coming home at night—it had to be at least ten thirty—from a regional speech and drama tournament in which we should have done well and didn't, all of us angry at one another and at ourselves. We'd have about a hundred miles to drive after we passed Dallas, and I hated the idea of being cooped up with these three for that long a time.

"We shouldn't have tried mime." I said it aloud, and Teena pounced.

"It was your brilliant idea, Lisa."

The car shuddered through a pothole in the road. I balanced myself, hanging on to the dashboard, and took a quick breath. "I thought all of you would practice until you had it right." I knew I was being mean, but I stared at Bo as I said it.

"It was a dumb idea," Bo said. "We looked like fools in those black turtleneck shirts and tights." Teena snorted, and Bo muttered, "I wouldn't have done it if Mrs. Lutz hadn't made me."

"You showed how you felt," Teena said. "Really must have impressed those judges. Yes, indeed."

"I don't care," Bo said. "I'm just glad my old man didn't see me." He jerked at the wheel as we hit a rut in the road. "Those tights aren't made for real men to wear. I didn't belong in that mime thing with the three of you."

I could hear Julian take a sharp breath, and I instinctively said, "Bo, don't be a nerd."

"Bo's a macho nerd," Teena said. "You know that Bo's daddy takes him out to a rifle range and teaches him to shoot to kill, in case the country comes apart and people are starving and some of them find out where Bo's family are all hid out in the hills with a house full of food?"

The car lurched and began to make sputtering noises. I don't know much about cars, but I could tell something was seriously wrong. This would be a terrible place to get stuck—out on the broad gully-gutted country north of Dallas, where sudden, rushing floods could turn dustland into lakes.

Bo made a fist and slammed it against the steering wheel. "Damn!" he said. "I just got this thing fixed last week." He turned to me. "Roll your window down and try to look out. See if there are any lights, any place we can stop for help."

We had passed some of the big spreads owned by Texas oil money and were coming into a section in which an occasional large home squatted in the middle of open acres, as though demanding breathing room.

I opened the side window as much as I dared, getting a blast of cold rain that stung my face. Quickly I rolled the window up and said, "There's a light ahead on the right. It looks as though the house is set back aways from the road. Do you think we can make it?"

He nodded.

"The road's underwater," I said.

"I know."

Bo nursed the car down the last patch of road toward the point of light that flickered through the rain-sopped windshield. He gentled the car off the road and into a long wide drive that curled upward to the front of the house. It was a huge old L-shaped house that stood on a rise, with a wide overhanging roof like a broad hat that shaded the two long wings. Near the angle in the "L" was a wide front door.

The engine in Bo's car gave a last shudder and died.

Bo leaned back against the vinyl seat and took a long breath, closing his eyes for a moment. He had a square, stocky face, a thick neck, and broad shoulders; and he seemed to be as popular in school as his father was in our town. Almost every week Mr. Elmer Baxter's picture was in the paper with a story saying he was being elected to an office in Rotary or Moose, or was doing something with the Clodine Civic Club.

A lot of the girls at school thought I was lucky to be working with Bo in speech and drama. I didn't think so, especially after I

[5]

found out he took the class only because he needed something he could pass in order to make grades and stay on the football team.

"So what do we do now?" Teena asked.

"Ring the doorbell," Julian said. His voice was quiet and calm, as though we were talking about who would pick up an order of burgers and fries. "My father belongs to the Automobile Club. If the people who live here let us use their phone, I'll call the club and ask them to send a tow truck to give us a lift into Dallas."

"We could phone our parents and tell them where we are," Teena said.

"We can do that later," Julian said. "They won't be expecting us in Clodine for hours. When we get into Dallas, we can let them know where we'll be until Bo's car is fixed."

"Maybe you're right," Teena said.

"Let's get with it," Bo said. "We'll have to run for the house."

We threw the car doors open, jumped out, slammed them, and sprinted toward the house, past a high four-wheel-drive Bronco in the drive, and up the steps to the porch. I shook my hair like a wet spaniel as we crowded under the overhang.

"Somebody's home," Teena said. "Their TV's on so loud it's blasting all the way out here."

"I hope they'll hear the doorbell," I said. Since I was nearest the door, I put out my finger to ring the bell.

At that moment the door flew open. The man standing there stared at us, looking about as bug-eyed as anyone could get. His thick black beard parted, and a strangling noise came out.

"We didn't mean to scare you," I said. "I was just going to ring your doorbell."

"Where did you come from?" His features seemed to draw together again, and the gap in his beard closed.

Bo stepped forward, crowding us against the door frame. "I'm Bo Baxter," he said. "My car broke down, and I managed to get it into your driveway."

"We're on our way home from a speech tournament," Teena said.

"And we saw your light," I added.

"I thought you kids went to those things in school buses," the man said.

"We usually do," I said, "except one of our

buses is out of commission, so they asked some of the kids to drive."

Julian stepped forward, nearly knocking me off the porch. He gripped my arm, holding me in place, and I was surprised at how strong he was for such a slender guy. "I'd appreciate it very much if you'd let us use your phone," Julian told the man. "I'd like to call the Automobile Club. We need help."

For a moment the man hesitated. He still looked a little dazed.

"If you'd prefer, I can give you my father's membership number, and you can make the call. We'll wait in the car," Julian said.

"No. No, the weather's terrible," the man said. "Come on inside. You can use the phone in the living room."

He stood aside, and we all tried to squeeze through the door at the same time. I dripped on a scatter rug by the front door and smiled nervously at Black Beard while Julian picked up a telephone that rested on a dark carved antique sideboard across the large room.

"What's your address?" Julian asked. When the man cupped one hand behind his ear, Julian repeated the question, yelling it this time.

"Uh—Cherry Road," Black Beard shouted. He looked blank.

"Twenty-two Cherry Road," Teena piped up. "I saw the numbers on the front porch."

"Yeah," Black Beard said.

"Could we turn down the television sound?" Julian shouted, and the man nodded, striding to the set and twisting the dial so fast the set snapped off with a sharp click.

"That's a relief," the man said. "I don't know why that was on so loud."

We must have really made him nervous, appearing under his nose like that. His clothes were rain-spattered. He had probably just come in and was going back out to the Bronco for something.

Julian nodded into the phone and kept nodding after he hung up. "I gave them the address and phone number. They'll send a mechanic and a tow truck as soon as they can get one here."

"Great," Teena snapped. "That could be tomorrow."

Julian just gave her a long, level glance. "They said the truck should be here in about half an hour."

Bo shrugged. "Okay. We can wait in the car."

I turned toward the door, but Black Beard said, "Wait a minute. It's real bad out there, isn't it?"

"It's raining hard," Bo said.

"You can wait in here," the man said. He quickly looked over his shoulder, then suddenly did it again. He laughed nervously as he realized we were staring at him.

Now it was my turn to feel squeamish. "Thank you, but I don't think we should," I said. This man was a stranger, and I felt uncomfortable in his house with my shoes squishing and rivulets from my long soggy hair trickling down my neck.

The others didn't move.

"Look, it's okay," the man said, as though he had just made up his mind about the whole thing. "You kids can watch television after my wife and I leave. Just be sure you lock the door when you go."

"After you leave?" Teena was first to react.

"Yeah. We have to—uh—go to a party," he said.

"But we can't stay in your house while you're not here!" I told him.

"You don't want to sit out in the rain," he answered. "Besides, the Auto Club might want to call you back or something, and you won't be here long. At least, I hope not." He looked over his shoulder again. It made me feel creepy.

"Since you don't mind," Julian said, "I think we'll do what you suggest, stay inside and watch television."

"Sure," Bo said. He looked down at Teena and me. "You girls will be safe with me here to protect you."

"Yeechh!" Teena made a face at him.

I had my mouth open to say something when we heard a faraway door slam and a mumbled curse. A woman's voice called, "Where are you?"

"In here," Black Beard shouted.

We could hear her moving toward us, her voice rapidly twanging like a flatted guitar string. "Let's get the hell out of here. We never should have come all that distance back. Something's all wrong. He's not here, and who cares that he left his jacket? I put it on a chair, and I—"

A tall, slim woman appeared in the archway that led to what I guessed must be the right wing of the house. Her jeans and faded T-shirt were as snug as lacquer on a fingernail

She stopped and stared at us. Then she stared at Black Beard. "Where did these kids come from?" she asked. Without waiting for an answer she glared at him and said, "Don't tell me you made another deal with hitchhikers."

"They're just some kids who had car trouble," he said. "They called the Auto Club, and I told them they could wait here."

For a moment she glared at him. The corners of her mouth twisted, and she snapped, "Mr. Impulsive again. Big heart? No way. I think it's zilch in the brains department. You had to—"

He interrupted her, his words spaced like firm stepping-stones, "We can't be late for the party."

"The party?" she said. "Are you crazy?"

"To go out in this weather?" he said. "No, because I promised we'd be there." He kept giving her the kinds of looks parents give each

[12]

other when they're trying not to be obvious and think you don't know they're talking over your head.

"But what about—? Did you look for—?"

"No need. He's gone by this time." Black Beard grabbed her elbow roughly, pulling her toward him. He steered her out the front door before we could say anything. "So long," he told us. "Don't forget to lock the door when you leave. It's got an automatic dead bolt." For some reason he gave that jittery laugh again.

The big front door thudded and clicked behind him.

"Who were they talking about?" I asked.

Teena looked at me. "*What* were they talking about? I don't think those space cadets knew if they were coming or going."

"You're right," I said. "Did you notice that their hair was damp? They had just got in from somewhere."

"Yeah. And what was all that phony stuff about a party? She didn't even know about any party."

"I don't understand why the television set was so loud," I said. "Neither one of them seemed to be hard of hearing."

"Y'all are too nosy," Bo said. He went straight to the television set and turned it on.

I could hear thunder rolling in the distance until the music came on strong and drowned it out. I was glad for something to erase that grumbling sound. I don't like storms in which lightning smacks the ground and the roar of thunder rattles in my head.

Julian sat on one of the flowered chintz chairs that faced the television. Teena walked to the window and back. "What we're doing is kinda crazy," she said. "I don't like being in a stranger's house."

"It feels weird," I said.

"Relax," Bo said. He stretched and slumped on the other flowered chair. A stiff crocheted doily surrounded his head like a starched halo. "We don't have a choice. Don't y'all want to sit down and watch Johnny Carson?"

"No," I said. I kept thinking about Black Beard and the woman and their weird conversation. My sweater began to smell like a warm, wet dog, so I pulled it off, tossing it on the throw rug near the front door.

"I'm hungry," Teena said. "Wish he'd told us to help ourselves to something to eat."

"You could skip a meal or two, and it wouldn't hurt you," Bo told her. "Being so little you probably only need to eat twice a week."

"Don't start anything," I said. I sat on the low brick ledge that jutted from the fireplace, resting my chin on my knees and hugging my legs. "We're all tired. We're upset because we didn't make the finals. We're saying things we don't mean."

"I'm not upset," Bo said, "and I sure as hell don't care that we didn't win. I'm only taking this class because the coach said I had to. My father didn't like the idea either, but I had to take something that would give me at least a solid B."

"I can understand a dumb jock looking for snap courses to make grades," Teena said. "But why would your father care if you took speech and drama? What's wrong with it?" She sat beside me on the bricks.

"You know," Bo said. He stared at the TV.

"I don't know," Julian said. His voice was a cold monotone. "Tell me."

Bo settled his shoulders into the back of his chair and looked at Julian. I looked at Julian, too. He was sitting as easily as a cat before a fire, but his hands were held down at his sides and knotted into tightly clenched fists.

"Face it," Bo said bluntly. "Most guys go out for sports, but some who can't make it in sports find other things they like even better, like acting and dancing and stuff."

"Yes?" Julian said.

Bo's voice became more hearty. "Like you guys are different, that's all. You probably want to go to New York and be on the stage someday. Right?"

"I'm going to be a doctor," Julian said.

Teena said, "With your daddy and your grandpa, there ought to be enough doctors in your family, Julian."

He answered quietly, "They want one more."

I was eager to change the subject. "How about you, Teena?" I asked. "What do you want to be?"

"Let's just say," Teena said, "that now we need a *black* woman on the Supreme Court."

"You want to be a lawyer?"

"Why not?" she said. "How about you, Lisa? What's your future?"

"I don't know. Right now I just want to make grades." Putting the thought into words was enough to make me feel a familiar pain in the middle of my stomach. Whenever I missed an answer on a test, when a paper came back saying something like "needs more work" or "room for improvement," the pain chewed at my gut. When my parents talked about the awards my brother and sister were getting in college or their achievements and how I would follow in their footsteps, I knew that pain well. I studied. Oh, how I studied! And all the time I was so scared.

I stood up, rubbing my midriff in a familiar gesture, as though I could rub the pain and the thoughts away.

"Where are you going?" Teena asked.

"I'm tired of sitting still," I said.

She and Julian and Bo went back to staring at Johnny Carson, who was staring at some actress in a dress that almost wasn't there.

I walked around the room, studying it. The furniture was old and expensive, the kind that grandmothers have had for a lifetime. My mother likes antiques, and I had learned enough from her to recognize a couple of really good pieces. The mahogany sideboard, with its carved legs and claw feet, gleamed with a patina of polish and care. The silver bowl of dying roses, with their yellowed, shriveled petals, rested at one end of the sideboard and was duplicated in a shadowy reflection. The room was somewhat cluttered with bric-a-brac, but even that seemed to be good stuff. Still, there was something strange about the room, something I couldn't quite put my finger on.

What am I trying to think of? I asked myself. *What is it?* Surprisingly, I was suddenly alert, a little afraid. I shivered.

[TWO]

THE THUNDER was closer, louder, and wind rattled the windows. I tried not to think of the storm. I reached back into my mind, tugging at the uncomfortable feeling that didn't want to come out, prying, pulling. And there it was. I spoke aloud. "That woman wasn't his wife."

Julian turned and stared at me. "What are you talking about?"

"She wasn't wearing a ring," I said. "And, anyhow, Teena and I don't believe they were going to a party, not in weather like this."

Bo snickered. "Look, the man said she was his wife. It's really none of our business."

"I don't care what Black Beard said."

Teena laughed. "Hey, Lisa, that's a good name for him. Old Black Beard!"

"I know she wasn't his wife," I insisted. "And another thing—he didn't tell us his name."

"I introduced us," Bo said. "He must have told us his name then." His forehead wrinkled. "Didn't he?"

"You only introduced yourself," Julian said. "Not us."

"It's kind of weird that he didn't tell us his name," Teena said. "That beard was weird, too, if you ask me. I wonder if it was for real."

"It was," I said.

"Yeah? What makes you so sure?"

"A real beard just looks different from a false beard," I said. "Unless an actor's awfully clever with a false beard, there's usually a tiny bit of spirit gum showing."

"Do you know much about acting?" Julian asked me. He wasn't being smart. He really seemed interested.

"Not very much," I said. "But when I was younger I was into magic tricks and disguises in a big way. I read everything I could find about magic and magicians. I even worked up a magic act, practiced like crazy, and was in some community shows." I laughed. "I wanted to be a magician more than I've ever wanted anything. I thought I'd try out for the Six Flags amusement park when I was old enough."

"And did you?"

"No," I said. "Being a magician takes too much time. I need all the time I can get to study." I realized it sounded as though I had memorized that line. Maybe I had.

"We're getting off the track," Teena said. "Lisa told us that Tight Pants wasn't Black Beard's wife, and I want to think about that some."

I walked to the windows. Through the sheer white curtains I could see intermittent flashes of sheet lightning. It was coming closer. The rain hammered loudly against the glass as the thunder growled.

I examined the folds of the flowered draperies that swathed each side of the windows. The fabric was soft and old and beautiful.

"Those people aren't the rose-brocade type," I said. "I'd be willing to bet anything that they wouldn't recognize an antique sideboard if they saw one with a price tag on it. They don't live in this house."

Bo stood up, turned off the TV set, and stretched. He shook his watch and scowled at it. "I wish that mechanic would get here," he said.

"Don't try to ignore what I said, Bo," I told him. "You know, too, that those people don't belong in this house. You're as eager to get out of here as I am, before the—" I stopped.

They all stared at me. "Before what?" Teena asked.

I moved a little closer to them, and what I said came out as a question. "Before the people who do live here get back and find us in their house?"

"You're just guessing," Bo said.

"Listen to me," I said, as I crossed the thick carpet to stand close to them. It was hard not to whisper, although there was no one else in the house to hear me. "Those people may have been in this house to rob it."

"They didn't seem to be taking anything," Julian said.

"That woman could have taken jewelry or money in her pockets."

"That woman couldn't have put anything

in her pockets," Bo said. He grinned at his own joke.

"There's something mighty funny here, all right," Teena said. She rubbed her chin as she talked. "That woman didn't have a handbag. No woman goes anywhere without something to carry her stuff in."

"Do you really think they were burglarizing the house?" Julian asked me.

"If the house didn't belong to them, they'd have to be burglars, wouldn't they?" Teena said. "What other reason would people have for being in houses where they don't belong?"

I shrugged. "Burglary...vandalism...spying...murder?"

Bo reached out and grabbed my arm, shaking me. "Cut it out, Lisa. The man invited us to stay here out of the rain. It isn't any of our business what he and that woman were doing, and the mechanic should get here any minute."

"You're letting your imagination get out of hand," Julian added.

"I was only—"

Bo spoke slowly, emphasizing the last word. "Don't be childish."

That hurt, but I wouldn't let him see it. I just shrugged. "I was only wondering what would happen to us if the people who live here get home before the guy from the Auto Club arrives. We could be arrested for trespassing. If those people have stolen something, the owners would think we did it."

Teena looked worried. "Lisa's got a point."

Julian shook his head. "The woman said something about their coming back because some guy forgot his jacket. She didn't act as though they'd been trying to burglarize the place."

"She asked if we were hitchhikers, too," I said.

"One big question," Teena said. "If they dropped some hitchhiker off here, where is he?"

"We're trying to piece together a situation on the basis of a few things the woman said that we don't understand," Julian said. "If whoever they were talking about were in this house, we'd have met him by this time. Right?"

"Right," Bo said. "Let's drop it. We'll be out of here soon, and none of this is our business."

"Okay, okay," Teena said. "I just want that

tow truck to come in a hurry, so we can get out of here."

They were probably right, but I still felt uncomfortable. I walked over to the sideboard. Maybe I should call my parents, after all. At least I'd hear a friendly voice.

I thought of my mom, and pictured her dashing through the house, pulling on her jacket, heading for the car. I smiled. Mom is probably the most active person in the Democratic party in the whole county. Dad keeps telling her she should run for office. Maybe someday she will—if she slows down enough. Dad's no slouch in politics, either. It's their way of trying to right wrongs, I guess, and they've always taken it for granted that their children would be just as bright and eager and active as they are.

My sister, Sharon, and my brother, Tom, are going to make my parents happy. They've collected scrapbooks full of honors, and they're going through law school with top grades. It's hard to follow a class act like that.

Teena followed me. "You got me jumpy, Lisa. What are we supposed to do now?"

"I don't know," I said. "I'm going to call

home. I think my mother will want to know where I am."

"Me after you," she said, and from the look she gave me I could tell she wanted the same reassurance I did.

The operator came on as soon as I finished dialing, and when a voice answered on the other end, she asked if they'd accept charges. I was awfully glad to hear my mother.

"Lisa?" she said in that vibrant, enthusiastic voice so great for making speeches. "Did you win, darling?"

"No," I said. "Mom—"

"Oh." Her tone was flat, but it picked itself up like a runner who trips near the finish line, and she said, "Next time then, honey bunch. This was a learning experience. Next time you'll be able to avoid today's mistakes."

I held a hand to my stomach, it was beginning to hurt.

Mom went right on. "Sharon called just a few minutes ago. She was chosen to be editor of the *Law Review*! Isn't that exciting?"

"That's great!" I tried to match her enthusiasm, but I couldn't make it. Before she got in another word I said as fast as I could, "Mom,

Bo's car broke down, and we're in someone's house waiting for the Auto Club."

There was a pause. "Are you sure you're all right? Who are these people?"

"I don't know their names. They had to leave."

"You don't know their names?"

I gave her the address and told her we were about a half hour out of Dallas. It wasn't my fault that I didn't know whose house we were in, but I felt stupid and guilty, as though I'd brought home an "F" in algebra.

"Do you want us to come and get you? Your father has a meeting to go to, but I think he could miss it."

"No, don't come," I said, wishing with all my heart they would. "It's raining awfully hard, and it would take you hours. The Automobile Club will be here soon."

"Lisa," Mom said, and then there was silence. We were cut off. There was no sound from the receiver at all.

"The phone's dead," I said, putting the receiver back on its cradle.

"What did you do to it?" Teena took the phone out of my hand and listened, then slammed it down on the sideboard and frowned.

Julian joined us. He held the receiver to his ear and jiggled the buttons on the cradle. Finally he said, "The phone is dead, but it's not Lisa's fault. Blame the storm."

Teena's voice was like a little girl's as she said, "I wish I could have called my mom."

I automatically opened my mouth to apologize, but before I could say anything she gave herself a little shake and picked up something on the sideboard. "Hey, look," she said. "A little guillotine. I've seen these in joke shops. Put your finger in here, ladies and gentlemen, and watch what happens!"

She reached for the string at the top of the guillotine, but didn't make it, because I grabbed her and shoved her away. The guillotine fell over on the sideboard.

"Hey!" Teena glared at me. "What was that all about?"

"You could have cut off your finger," I said.

Her eyes grew wide. "Come on, Lisa. It's just a toy."

"Is it? Watch." I pulled one of the roses from the nearby vase, put the guillotine in place, laid the stem across the wooden block at the bottom of the guillotine, and pulled the string. The guillotine blade neatly sliced the rose stem in two.

Teena stepped away, rubbing her finger. "How did you know it would do that?"

"I told you. I'm a magician. I saw this when I was looking around. It's too well made to be a toy. It's got to be a piece of professional equipment. Look at the wood in this. Look at the steel in the blade. I've heard of magicians who use something like this for smaller tricks, then bring in the large ones and have their assistants put their necks on the block."

"Ugh!" Teena said.

Julian picked up the guillotine and examined it carefully.

"It's not dangerous when it's done properly," I told them. "There's a safety catch that the audience can't see."

I didn't want to think about what could have happened to Teena's finger. I looked around the room. "I wonder if there are any other things in here that a magician would use."

"I haven't seen any," Julian said.

"Do you think the person who lives here is a magician?" Teena asked.

"I don't know."

"This is a big house," Teena said. "Maybe there's more magic stuff in the other rooms."

"If you're going to suggest looking in the other rooms, my suggestion is, forget it," Julian told her.

"Okay, okay. I'm with you," Teena said quickly. "I just want to get out of this place."

Bo opened the front door, letting in a blast of cold air and rain.

"Close that!" Teena and I yelled at him.

He pushed the door shut, working against the wind. The door seemed to shiver as the dead bolt slid into place, and a clean smell, like cold steel, sliced through the stale, decaying rose fragrance in the room.

"The water's rising," Bo said. "I'm worried about my car."

"How about our stuff in the trunk?" Teena said. "Can we bring it inside?"

"I'll get it," Julian said.

I stepped forward. "I'll help."

Bo shook his head. "Y'all stay inside. Julian and I will get it."

The two of them hurried out the door. Teena pushed it shut, cutting off the blast of rain. She giggled. "Sometimes macho comes in handy. I'd rather stay inside than go out in that."

Bo and Julian were back in minutes. They dropped our four small cases near the door. "It's like a damn river out there," Bo said, shaking the water from his hair.

"There's a good-sized rise up to the house from the drive," Julian said. "Unless the storm dumps an awful lot more rain the house shouldn't flood."

Teena turned on the television set. "Maybe we ought to keep this on in case there's a flash-flood warning."

She huddled in a chair close to the set; but I walked around the room, over the thick carpet and a faded Oriental rug with a raspberry red scroll motif. I couldn't sit still. I peered through the old-fashioned archway the woman had come through and saw a long hallway. There was enough light from the living room to show that the right side of the hall opened into a large dining room with an ornate table and stiff, formal chairs. Undoubtedly, a kitchen was somewhere down the hall beyond the dining room. The house seemed to sprawl and spread in two directions, like a V, as far as I could tell.

At the far end of the living room, on my left, there was another archway, a smaller one, and I was drawn to it. It was a gate into darkness. In the dim light reflecting from the living-room lamps I could just make out doors along the hallway, but they were shut. Only one—the door at the far end of the hall—stood open.

There was a special kind of darkness in that hallway. I could feel it creep around me. I listened, and it was as though those rooms were free of the noise of the storm outside, even free of the chatter on the television. The silence in those black rooms was unbearable.

I half turned to Julian, who was still studying the little guillotine. "I think someone is back there," I told him.

Julian came to stand beside me. "You heard someone?"

I shook my head quickly. "I didn't hear a thing."

"Then why do you think someone is there?"

"Because it's a strange kind of quiet." I took a deep breath. "I know it sounds crazy, but I feel as though someone is in one of those rooms."

Julian was looking at me oddly, so I tried to explain. "Don't you ever come home and know the moment you open the door whether someone in your family is there or not?"

"I guess I've never thought about it," he answered, but he looked down the hall. "Do you mean you think the hitchhiker, whoever he was, is back there?"

"I don't know." I shivered. I took his hand and realized that my fingers were freezing. "Julian," I whispered, "I know this is just a feeling, but it's scaring me to death!"

"I still think that if someone were in this house, we'd know it."

It was the first thing that came into my mind, and without thinking I blurted out, "Unless it's someone who's no longer alive!"

[THREE]

THERE HAD been a lull in the sound from the television, so my words were overloud. They hung in the stillness like echoes before they slid away.

Teena was on her feet. "Cut that out, Lisa!" she cried. "Stop trying to scare us!"

The raucous laughter that suddenly burst from the television set was so out of place that Bo reached over and turned down the sound.

"Where's that damn mechanic?" he muttered. He came to join us, Teena scampering after him. He kept his eyes on me, but the others stared into the dark hallway. We were all frightened.

I tried to explain. "Don't you ever feel like someone's sending you a mental message? That's what ESP is all about, and I've always been good at ESP. When I was just five years old and my aunt Sarah died over in Lubbock, I saw her, and I told my mother, and—"

"I don't want to hear about it!" Teena clapped her hands over her ears.

For a moment we simply looked at each other. A splat of bright light outlined the windows, and I automatically counted, "One one thousand, two one thousand, three one thousand, four—" before thunder shuddered through the house. "It's closer," I said. "Less than four miles away."

The loud pounding on the door was so surprising that we all jumped. Teena let out a shriek.

"The Auto Club!" Bo said, his voice heavy with relief.

I gave one quick glance over my shoulder down the dark hallway and followed the others to the door. Bo pulled the door open, and a stocky figure plowed into the room, head down, shedding water on the scatter rug. When she looked up, I saw a woman with weather-toughened skin and broad shoulders.

She pulled off a shiny yellow rain hat while her deep blue eyes mapped our faces. "Who are y'all? Where's Miz Gracie Ella?"

"We don't even know a Mrs. Gracie Ella," I said.

"Then what are y'all doin' in her house?"

"Is Mrs. Gracie Ella young with dark hair?" Julian asked.

"Nothin' like that," she said, so he told her about the car trouble and the man and woman who invited us to wait out of the rain until the Auto Club mechanic would arrive.

"That tow truck may have a time gettin' through," she said. "Lots of stalled cars down to the expressway." She studied us again. "Tell me more about those people who let you in."

"The man was tall with a black beard," I said. "And the woman was young. She was pretty, in a way."

"Can't say I've ever seen either of them," she said, "Far as I know they've never been here, and I don't know why they'd be here now if Miz Gracie Ella wasn't. And it looks like she had enough sense to stay put in Dallas and not try to drive home in this."

She nodded as though she were shaking her thoughts into place. "Caught sight of your car out there," she said. "First off I thought it was Miz Gracie Ella's car, till I got up close. She told me she was goin' into Dallas this mornin' for shoppin'. Didn't know it was goin' to rain so bad this mornin'." She looked at each of us in turn. "I check on her a lot, since she lives alone and her arthritis is gettin' worse. She don't have any relations to care about her. At least not since her sister in New Jersey died sudden near a month ago. And at that she hadn't seen her sister for years, although they kept in touch regular. Didn't even get up to her sister's funeral."

I thought about the back room, but hesitated to tell her what I had told the others. Would she think I was weird? After all, it was only a feeling I'd had. "Do you think she might be somewhere in the house?" I asked.

"If she was in the house she'd be right here at the door to see who it was. Her hearin's not what it could be, but I figure you kids haven't exactly been tiptoein' around. Yep. She'd be climbin' out of her bed to see what's what." I must have looked puzzled, because she added, "She turns in early in the evenin' and gets up before it gets light."

Her eyes narrowed as she thought. "She must still be in Dallas. There's a little hotel she stays at sometimes when she don't want to drive back the same day."

Her reassurance was so welcome I clung to it like a security blanket. But I realized we were still standing by the door, and I waved toward the chairs in the living room. "Don't you want to sit down?" I asked. "Miss...Mrs....?"

"Lonnie Whitt," she said. "And, no, I don't want to sit down. Not in these wet clothes. I live down the road a piece, and it's time I got home."

She walked over to the phone, picked up the pad and pencil that lay near it, and motioned to us.

"Write down your names and addresses," she said. "Since that's your car in the drive I'll fix the license number in my head."

We must have looked surprised, because she added, "Well, y'all don't belong in this house, you gotta admit."

Julian was first to respond. "You're right," he said. He joined her, reached for the pad, and wrote down the information she wanted. We all did the same.

My glance fell on the guillotine. "Is Mrs. Gracie Ella a magician?" I asked.

Lonnie Whitt saw what I was looking at and said, "Not her. It was her husband who did all that magic stuff. You ever hear of 'Chamberlain the Great'?"

We must have looked blank, so she added, "I didn't think so. I guess he was in show business for years. She said he was real well known back East, but I never heard of him. Miz Gracie Ella bought this house with the insurance money and moved here two years ago, after he died. It was a real tragic thing—a big fire in a theater where he was puttin' on his show. They found what was left of his body after the fire got put out. She just up and moved here to the Dallas area, and brought most of his magic stuff with her in that trailer they used when they traveled around, puttin' on shows."

"Why'd she come all the way to Texas?" Teena asked.

"I dunno. Might be the cold up there got to her. She's not as young as she once was."

I thought about Chamberlain the Great's magic props. "I'd like to meet Mrs. Chamberlain," I said.

"It's not Chamberlain. That was her husband's stage name. Her last name is Porter, and she's not very sociable," Lonnie said. "I probably see more of her than anybody, and that's only because, as I said, I try to keep an eye on her, with her livin' alone and all that. Don't even know if she likes my pokin' around, because lately she's been keepin' pretty much to herself; but I feel it's my Christian duty to check on her now and then."

"You seem to know a lot about her," I said.

"Just what I find out when I ask questions," she said. "I figure, us bein' neighbors, there's certain things we should know about each other, and I'm not goin' to know unless I come right out and ask." She cocked her head like a banty rooster as she looked at me. "And speakin' of askin' questions, why are you so eager to meet her?"

"I just thought that maybe someday she'd

be willing to show me her husband's equipment," I said.

She seemed surprised. "It looks like most magician stuff, I'd guess."

"Magicians are inventors," I told her. "They have to keep surprising their audiences, so they try to invent new tricks and new ways of doing old tricks. They often build some of their own equipment."

"Lisa is a magician," Teena said.

I smiled at her. I loved the sound of those words, and I don't remember anyone ever saying them before.

Lonnie shrugged. "Well, sometime maybe Miz Gracie Ella might show you the stuff. Don't know why not. There's boxes big enough to hold bodies, or stick swords through, all of that."

"Is it stored away?"

"Naw. She kept it in their fancy trailer for a while, but for some reason last month she sold the trailer. Had the people who bought it move all that magician stuff inside. It's in that big room between the two hallways."

I spoke my thought. "I wonder why she's kept the equipment, since she's not a magician."

She grimaced. "Girl, you're not the only one who's wondered. I told her I wished she'd get rid of it. She won't tell me why, but for some reason she seems scared not to keep it."

"I wouldn't want that creepy magician stuff around my house," Teena said.

"You're right. It's not healthy. Makes her think about her husband. And from what little she's said about him, he wasn't worth thinkin' about. He must have been a mean old devil. Why, one time me and her were havin' a little drink together—iced tea for me, of course, although Miz Gracie Ella was havin' somethin' a lot stronger—and she got started talkin' about how cruel he was to people. He liked to tease them on and on until bam! He got them. Like the young feller Chamberlain made to think he was goin' to get hired as his apprentice, and he got him to working harder and harder for him—without payin' him, of course—until one night they just up and moved without ever lettin' the young feller know. And there was a stagehand he kept urgin' to ask for a raise, but he'd been talkin' lies behind the feller's back to the theater manager, and when the stagehand asked for his raise he got bawled out and fired. Chamberlain thought it was funny."

I shivered, and Teena said, "I'd never want to meet him!"

"Alive or dead, that old man scares Miz Gracie Ella," Mrs. Whitt said. "I'm just glad she's never tried to call up his spirit."

The others must have looked as startled as I felt, because she laughed. "Didn't mean to scare y'all. I guess I forgot to say Miz Gracie Ella's a medium. When she first came to these parts she painted that room I told y'all about black, even on the ceiling, and fixed it up with a round table and some chairs and candles and held what she said was 'readings' to call up dead relations for people."

"Does she still do it?" I asked. "Did you ever go to any of her sessions?"

"Of course not," Lonnie told me. "I'm a regular churchgoer and don't hold that with nonsense." She chuckled. "Neither does the sheriff. He had a little talk with her, and told her there were laws against trickin' people and chargin' them for it, so she decided to retire. Never used that séance room again, far as I know, until she moved the magician stuff into it."

[44]

She pinned us once again with those steady blue eyes. "I suppose I ought to stay here until that fella from the Auto Club comes and make sure you kids leave the house all right."

A gust of rain slammed against the roof, and she had to raise her voice. "Nope. I'd better get on home. If the water should rise up into the house like it done ten years ago, I'll have to start movin' things on top of tables."

I thought about that dark hallway and what she had told us about the woman who lived in this house. I stepped closer to her, my words spilling out eagerly. "Could we go with you?"

"We can't do that," Bo said. "We have to wait for the mechanic." He looked at an invisible spot on the wall over Lonnie's head. "And I think we ought to stick together."

"Hey, big jock, you'd be scared here by yourself?" Teena grinned at him.

"The boy is right," Lonnie said. "Y'all don't know any more about me than I know about you. Except remember I've got your names and addresses, and I'll be givin' 'em to the sheriff, along with that information about the people who let you in here. Since y'all seem like honest kids, that ought to be okay."

She paused, and we all nodded in agreement. She looked satisfied. "If the phone don't work, I've got the CB."

She pulled on the yellow hat, tucking in stray wisps of hair. "There's candles and matches in the sideboard over there," she said. "Probably more in the kitchen, too. Better get some ready in case we lose the electricity."

She tugged the big door open and shoved herself into the wind. A flash of lightning outlined her stocky body as she ran toward her pickup truck.

Bo pushed the door shut. We all stared at each other. Finally I couldn't stand it. "What do we do now?" I asked.

Bo looked at his watch. Then he shook his wrist and looked at the watch again. "The Auto Club should have been here by now," he said.

"So we wait," Teena said.

I thought about the room filled with the magician's equipment. "I'd love to see some of Chamberlain the Great's things," I said. "Do you think it would be all right?"

Julian frowned. "We shouldn't prowl through Mrs. Gracie Ella's house."

"It wouldn't be prowling," I answered. "Not

if I just look at the equipment. Lonnie Whitt told us that most of it was in a room off the hallway."

"Could you do some of the tricks for us?" Teena asked.

"Most of the tricks—the big ones, like running swords through someone inside a box—take an assistant. She has to be somebody small and flexible enough to get into a small space."

"I'm small and flexible," Teena said. "I didn't know there was a market for it."

"We can look, but we shouldn't touch the Great Chamberlain's equipment. It wouldn't be ethical."

"I don't think I'd like to try that sword thing anyway," Teena said. "What if I were in the box and one of those swords slipped?"

"It's all an illusion," I said.

"You mean those things aren't real?"

"Oh, they're all real," I told her. "It's just the way it's done. A magician tries to make his audience believe they are seeing something they aren't. It's an illusion. Magicians call themselves illusionists."

"Let's all sit down," Julian said. "This isn't our house, and we shouldn't leave this room."

"Who put you in charge?" Bo asked.

"He's going to be a doctor, like his daddy and his granddaddy." Teena giggled. "He has to practice being in charge of things. Don't you watch TV, Bo? Don't you know doctors are always in charge of things?"

"I know one thing about doctors," Bo said. He ambled over to the big chair in front of the television set and settled into it, stretching his long legs out in front of him. "They don't take ballet lessons."

Julian stood in front of Bo. His body was so tense it was as taut as a cello string, and I thought, *Julian moves like a dancer. He's graceful.*

"What I enjoy doing is none of your business," Julian told Bo.

"Hey, look," I said, quickly stepping between them and taking Julian's arm. "Don't be upset. Teena was just kidding, and Bo didn't mean anything either."

Julian didn't say anything. He kept his eyes on Bo's face. I walked over and sat on the arm of Bo's chair. "We're tired, and we're scared, and we're taking our feelings out on each other," I said.

Bo snorted and stuck out his chin. "Scared of what?"

"Scared of where we are and what's going to happen to us," I said. "Don't tell me you're not afraid."

"Being afraid is a waste of energy."

"Aw, Bo, even you are scared sometimes."

"He can't admit it," Teena said. "It would ruin his image as macho man."

"So now you're a psychiatrist? I thought you were going to be a big, famous lawyer," Bo drawled.

Teena turned and walked to a nearby sofa, pulling Julian with her. "The lawyer job is the plan, man," she said. "It's what my mama and daddy have got their hearts set on."

Julian turned to look at her. "What about you? Is that what you want?"

Teena shrugged. "I don't know what I want."

"That's pretty ambitious for your parents to want you to be a lawyer," Bo told her. "Don't they work in Bundy's Café?"

"You know where they work," Teena snapped, "because you and that jock crowd are always hanging around Bundy's. And, anyhow, that has nothing to do with what they want for me."

The bickering was making me uncomfortable. I tried to ease the situation. "Teena, I bet you'll be a good lawyer," I said. "You've got a sharp mind."

Teena relaxed, but she didn't look very happy. "Sometimes I think my parents are sort of like the Kennedys," she said.

Bo snorted again, and I dug my fingers into his shoulder.

"Ow!" he said, sitting upright and knocking my hand away. "What was that for?"

"Shut up," I told him. "I want to hear what Teena's saying."

"It's just that my parents wanted something special for their first child," Teena said. "Like Joe and Rose Kennedy wanted the presidency for theirs. Only my brother joined the army and got killed in a truck crash in the desert. So they turned all their hopes on my sister, Connie. But Connie ran away."

"I'm sorry," I said.

Teena shook her head. "Connie's happy,"

she said. "She's married and she's got two babies, and she's real happy."

"So now it's you they're counting on," Julian said.

She nodded. None of us said anything. Maybe they were thinking the same kinds of thoughts I was thinking about parents and plans and futures. Maybe the plans came with the labor pains. And what happened to kids who didn't live up to the plans? My childhood had a lot of happy moments, with Mom and Dad doing things with us, having fun with us. But there were always the things they expected, and my memories were mixed up with urgent desires to please my parents.

"Lisa, why don't you enter the swimming competition? When Tom was your age we couldn't get him out of the pool, and he won all the blue ribbons."

"Lisa, we know you're going to be the very best pianist in the recital tonight!"

"Lisa, what's this 'B' in history? Was there some problem with the teacher? We know you can get an 'A' with just a little effort."

"You're going to have work harder if you want

to go for the scholarships, Lisa. Sharon and Tom won them, and there's no reason why you can't, too."

I was beginning to get that pain in my stomach again when I heard the noise.

[FOUR]

IT WAS such a small noise that at first I held my breath, waiting, wondering if I had really heard it, and if it would come again. A footstep? Someone brushing against something? Or could it have been my imagination? The thunder was growling its way toward the east, but the rain made a constant drumming.

I hadn't been the only one who heard the sound. Julian was alert, staring toward the archway to the hall. Teena had a hand up to her mouth, and her eyes were wide.

"What was it?" I whispered.

"I don't know." Julian's voice was low. "I don't even know what direction it came from. Do you?"

"What are y'all talking about?" Bo asked so loudly that I jumped.

"There was a sound somewhere in the house," I whispered. I stood, facing that dark hallway across the room. Maybe I expected someone to step from it. I don't know. I was waiting for someone—something.

Bo stood, too, and held up a hand. "Y'all be quiet," he said. "Listen. I hear a truck coming."

Unmistakably there was the sound of an engine in front of the house. With one accord we raced to the front door.

Bo yanked it open in time for a tall, lanky figure in a black plastic raincoat to dash into the room. He shook himself and said, "Y'all called the Auto Club? I'm Sam."

"Are we glad to see you!" Teena said.

"It's the car on the drive," Bo said. "I think it's the carburetor. If you could get it started—"

"No way," Sam said. "I can't work on it in this downpour. Best I can do is tow it in."

"Can we drive back to the city with you?" Teena asked.

"Not all of you," Sam said. "My cab only holds two passengers." No one spoke. He glanced at each of us in turn. "Well? Two of you want to come along?"

I wanted to get out of that house, but instead of shouting, "Take me!" I found myself saying, "Bo told us that we should all stick together. I think he's right."

Julian frowned. "This storm could get worse. I think you and Teena should go with Sam into town. You can make arrangements for someone to pick up Bo and me after the rain is over and the water goes down."

"Yeah," Bo said, sticking out his chest and looking like Superhero in the cartoons. "That makes sense. We'll have to take care of the girls."

"I'll get y'all's car hooked up," Sam said. "The little girls can make a run for the cab. Door's unlocked."

I glanced toward the hallway. "Wait a minute," I said. "I don't think we should leave Julian and Bo before we take a look in that hallway—especially in the back room with the open door."

Bo whirled and snapped at me, "Nobody's in that room!"

"Huh?" Sam turned and stared at us.

"Maybe it's just the way I feel. Maybe it's because of a sound we heard, but I keep wondering if someone besides us is in this house."

"We better explain," Julian said. "This isn't our house. A man and his wife let us in out of the rain and—"

"She wasn't his wife," Teena said.

"It makes no difference," Julian said. "They invited us to stay here while they went to a party."

"That doesn't sound right," Sam said.

"I know it seems weird," I told him, "but that's how it happened." Sam didn't say anything, and I added, "Look, we don't like the situation either. We've been wondering what would happen if the people who lived here came home and found us in their house."

"I thought you said they invited you in."

"We don't think they live here."

"Is this a trick, or what?" Sam asked. He took another step backward, toward the door.

"Just get going!" Bo said, grabbing my arm. "Okay?"

Sam raised a hand. "Hold it," he said to Bo,

but he looked at me. "Y'all think someone's in the house. Whoever it is must be layin' low. Why?"

"I don't know," I said. I didn't want to tell Sam what I had sensed. I couldn't tell him how frightened I was.

Julian stepped in. "The people said something about a hitchhiker."

"Where's the hitchhiker?"

"We don't know that either," Teena said.

"But we think we heard a noise in the direction of the last room on the hallway," I said.

"So go take a look," Sam said. "I'll wait."

No one moved.

"We haven't got all day." Sam shouldered past us and stomped into the hallway. "Light's burnt out," he muttered as he flipped the switch up and down.

We stood in a tight cluster by the front door as Sam went down the hallway. We could hear him opening doors, turning lights on and off, and shutting doors again as he moved toward the end of the hall.

I found myself walking alone toward the archway, drawn to the hallway, holding my breath as I waited for Sam to reach that last room.

I heard him bump something as he fumbled for the light switch. As a patch of light spread into the end of the hall, Sam gave a gasping, guttural cry. He backed into the hall, turned, and staggered toward us, his face distorted by the shadows, and his eyes glittering.

"No!" he said. "There's—"

He suddenly reached out both arms to clutch at me, but his eyes rolled up, and he fell, dragging me with him.

I thought it was Teena who was screaming, but I felt myself being pulled to my feet, and Bo was shouting, "Stop that, Lisa!"

"I'm sorry!" I couldn't stop shaking, and I clung to Bo, trying to catch my breath.

Teena clutched my arm. "What happened to him? Is he dead?"

Julian loosened Sam's collar. "He's okay," Julian said. "His pulse is strong, and so is his heartbeat. He just fainted."

"Why?" Bo asked.

Julian got to his feet, and the three of them stared at me, waiting for an answer.

"I don't know," I said. "He saw something in

that last room that scared him, I guess." I looked down the hallway, and the room was dark.

Had he left the light on? I'd thought so, but I'd been so frightened. How could I remember something like that?

"What do we do now?" Teena whispered.

"I'm going to find the kitchen and get some water and a towel," Julian said. "Sam will come out of his faint eventually, but I want to speed it up. Maybe you haven't noticed, but judging from the thunder there's another wave of the storm coming toward us."

I realized the thunder was louder. "I'll go with you," I told him. "The kitchen must be in the wing beyond the dining room."

We found the light switch in the hall opposite the dining room, and it was just light enough for us to see. Small, dim bulbs in an old wall sconce. By the time we had entered the hallway, Teena was between us.

"I'm coming, too," she said.

There was an open door to the left.

"The magic room?" I whispered. The room was dark, but light spilled in and across familiar boxes. There was no mistaking the magic prop near the door.

"Look at that table!" I said. "It's even covered with one of those old velvet gold-fringed cloths!"

Teena tugged at my arm. "We haven't got time for you to look at that stuff. Keep moving."

We opened doors to a narrow butler's pantry next to the dining room. On the same side of the hall was an empty room with an inside door to a small bathroom that must have been meant for servants' quarters, and beyond that room was a crowded garage with boxes piled up practically to the car. Finally, thankfully, on our left was the kitchen.

It was a huge old-fashioned room, with brown-stained wooden cabinets and a large wooden table in the center. The table and chairs had once been painted an apple green and were faded now to a sickly color. There was a stale smell of bacon grease, and a couple of dirty dishes on the edge of the sink.

But my glance was pulled toward the back door. A chair had been shoved against it, holding it almost shut. Rain was seeping through the crack and under the door, making a cold, shiny puddle on the worn linoleum floor.

Around the lock on the door the wood had been splintered away.

"They did break into the house!" Teena shouted. "Black Beard and the woman! They were here to burglarize the house!"

"And we interrupted them," Julian added.

"Oh, my gosh!" Teena said. "We've got to call the police!"

"On what?" I said. "Remember? The phone is dead."

But Teena had run to a wall phone and was frantically clicking the button up and down. When she finally hung up she looked sick. "We're witnesses," she said. "They could have killed us."

"But they didn't," I said.

"Why are you frowning at me?" Teena demanded.

"I'm not frowning at you," I told her. "I'm trying to think. Where does the hitchhiker fit in?"

For an instant they stared at me blankly. Then Teena said, "Yeah. We're back to the hitchhiker."

Julian said, "That woman told the man

with the beard that they shouldn't have come back, that there was something wrong here."

"But they were bringing the man his jacket," Teena said. "So maybe they dropped him off on the road, and he said he was coming here, and when they realized he left his jacket in the car, they came back here to give it to him."

"Obviously he didn't let them in," I said.

"They could hear the TV on loud," Teena said, so they knew he was home and probably couldn't hear them at the door.

"And they found the back-door lock broken," Julian said.

"I wonder what they thought?" Teena said.

"They probably wanted to get out of here in a hurry," I said. "Remember, Black Beard was coming out the front door just as we arrived on the porch? And he didn't seem any too happy about being in this house."

"Why'd the hitchhiker do this to the back door? Why didn't he just break in the front door?" Teena asked.

"Look," I said. "No dead bolt on this door. The front door has a dead bolt on it."

"Do you think he stole something from this house and left?"

"Maybe," I said. "But why did he pick this particular house?"

Julian was looking around the room. "Didn't that woman say something about leaving the jacket on a chair? I didn't see a jacket in here."

"Maybe she left it in another room," Teena said.

"What other room?" I asked. "She came from this direction, remember?"

"Then where's the jacket?"

None of us said anything. I'm sure we were all afraid to put our thoughts into words.

"What's keeping y'all?" Bo came up behind us. He stopped when he saw the back door. "Hey, Lisa, you were right," he said.

"I thought you were staying with Sam," Julian told him.

"Y'all didn't come back. I didn't want—that is, I thought you might need help, so I came looking for you to see what happened."

Teena made a face. "That's real good of you, Bo."

Julian hurried to the counter and began rummaging through the nearest drawers until he found a dish towel. He ran cold water over it, wrung it out, and hurried back to the living room. We were following him so closely that when he suddenly stopped, I bumped into him and Teena plowed into me. Bo let out a yelp.

"He's gone!" Julian said.

All I could do was gasp.

The front door was open, and rain was blowing through. We scrambled past each other, trying to reach the door, crowding together, pushing, shoving, in order to see.

"He's gone off with his damn truck!" Bo yelled.

"I told you to stay with him," Julian shouted.

"Then why in hell didn't you come back?" Bo groaned and leaned against the door frame. "Look at my car! The water's so high it's inside it!"

"Why did Sam go without us?" Teena wandered over to the nearest chair and dropped into it. "He said he'd take us with him."

I tugged at the door, elbowing Julian and Bo out of my way, and slammed it. "Think about it," I said. I tried to dry the rain from my face with the sleeve of my blouse. "Sam saw something that scared him so much he fainted. Then he came to, and we had disappeared. He wouldn't know we were in the kitchen. He was probably scared to death of *us*. All he knew was that he had to get out of this place."

"Maybe he'll go for the police," Julian said.

"I hope so," Teena murmured. Her voice squeaked as though she were trying not to cry.

I would have liked to comfort her. I would have loved it if someone had tried to comfort me. All I could do was lean against the door, hoping it would hold me. My legs were wobbly. My mind seemed to tremble as much as my body, but one thought came through clearly. "Whatever Sam saw," I said, "is still in this house. And like it or not, we're trapped in here with it."

[FIVE]

"IT'S YOUR fault, Lisa," Bo said. "Why'd you have to say what you did? You and Teena would have been out of here by this time."

I shuddered. "I'm scared, too," I said.

It hit a nerve. "We're not talking about being afraid!" he shouted at me. "We're talking about what should have happened, Lisa!"

Bo's face was wet with rain. I stooped down to the pile of cases on the floor, zipped mine open, and took out a couple of tissues. Then I held his chin, as I would a little child's, and dried his face. He let me, as though he didn't notice what I was doing. My hands stopped shaking. It helped me more than it helped him.

"I guess I had to say it," I told him. "It was just the feeling that someone might be in that room."

He took a step forward, brushing my hand away. "Then go look and find out for yourself. Go on, Lisa."

Julian took my arm and steered me into the nearest chair. He settled on the floor next to me. "Lisa isn't going into that room. None of us is."

"Why not?" Bo sneered at Julian. "Making the rules again?"

"Don't anybody go in that room!" Teena said. "Look what happened to Sam! He wouldn't have acted like that if he just saw somebody sick in bed or a little kid. If there's somebody in that room, they sure don't need us."

Bo had raised his head and was staring at the television set. "Warning from the National Weather Bureau," he read slowly as the words appeared across the bottom of the screen. We all scrambled toward the set. Bo turned up the sound so we could hear what the newscaster behind the desk was saying.

"Flash flooding in the following counties," he announced, and his voice droned on.

"What county is this?" I asked Julian.

He shrugged. "It doesn't matter. It's undoubtedly one of those getting the floods."

"The warning's a little late." Teena glared at the set.

"What am I going to do about my car?" Bo mumbled.

I knew he was talking to himself, but Teena said, "Tell your daddy to just go out on his big car lot and get you another one."

"I had to earn that car!" Bo snapped.

"Yeah? I didn't know you ever had any kind of job, big jock. I thought all you did was play football."

"That's how I earned it. I made the team." Bo answered so softly that Teena dropped her mocking tone.

"You mean it? Your car was a reward?"

"It's a big thing for my old man," Bo said. "He's always gone to all the Friday night school football games. Used to play in high school himself."

"Was he good?" I asked.

Bo shook his head. "He didn't make first string until his last semester, and then didn't cut it. He said he wasn't tall and heavy enough.

It really killed him. He wanted more than anything to play football in college."

"So now you're playing for him," Julian said.

"What difference does it make?" Bo asked. "I'm not that great in the brains department. So there's not much else to do. Football's okay."

"I heard you got some scholarship offers," Julian said.

Bo looked surprised. "Yeah. USC and Washington State. Michigan, too. They came through, but Dad wants me to go with Texas."

"So he can go to all the games," Teena said. "Bo, don't you ever want to see new places? Something better than our little old Clodine?"

Bo didn't answer, but Julian said, "I wish I could go to New York to study."

"You want to be a doctor in New York?" Bo asked.

"I'm going to be a doctor, but I want to be a dancer," Julian said.

"I just want to get away," Teena said. "I don't know where."

The house vibrated as a clap of thunder struck. I shivered.

"What I want right now," I said, "is a bathroom."

"Me, too," Teena said. We instinctively looked toward the hallway, and she added, "Oh, no! I'm not going in there to look for a bathroom."

"There's a room near the kitchen," I said. "Remember that empty room? I think there's a small bathroom there, too."

"You want us to walk down there with you?" Julian asked, but I shook my head.

"It's okay. We'll just turn on all the lights."

Teena and I went past the dining room and through the hallway that led to the kitchen. At the open door to the magic room I stopped. I reached inside and felt for the light switch, flipping the room into a dim glow.

"Stay out of there, Lisa!" Teena said. She tugged at my arm.

I gasped, staring into the room. It was not a large room, but the walls were a flat, dull black and, in the dim light, seemed to stretch out into the night. It was like being swallowed by a huge, black mouth. Trunks and boxes lined the walls. Near us was an ornate, wide thronelike chair, facing the door. Next to it was a large cube-shaped box with swords lying on top.

Teena had stopped pulling at me. She was beside me, her face close to my shoulder. "So that's where Mrs. Gracie Ella gave psychic readings," she whispered. "I guess her customers would believe anything scary in a room like this."

I nodded and she added, "What's that thing? Is that one of those tricks where the magician sticks swords through somebody?"

"He pretends to," I said.

"You know how to do that?"

I nodded, and Teena let out a low whistle. "How about that fancy chair? What's that for?"

"Let's go in and I'll tell you about some of them," I said. "There are some things in here I know, and some I've never seen before."

"No," Teena said. "No way. Not unless we're all together." She pushed me toward the hallway. "Let's find that bathroom. We can come back here with the others."

"Wait a minute," I said. "See that door on the left side?"

"What door?"

"It's hard to make out, because of that ugly black paint, but there's a door over there."

I could hear her take a quick breath. "What about it?"

"It must open into one of the rooms along the bedroom hallway. You could go through this room into a room along that hall without going into the dining room or living room. Mrs. Whitt said this room was between the two hallways, and now I see what she meant."

"Lisa!" Teena's voice was sharp. "Get out of here!" She reached over and turned off the light. I followed her past the butler's pantry to the empty room, both on the right of the hallway in line with the dining room. There was a bulb in the overhead lamp, but it was dim, too.

"Somebody in this house sure doesn't want to waste money on lights to see by," Teena said. We crossed the room to the door on the other side and turned on another forty-watt bulb in a small, white-tiled bathroom.

"You first," Teena said. I just stood there, looking at the empty bedroom, and she said, "Mind if I come in with you?"

As I washed my hands I peered into the mirror over the small basin. "I wish I'd brought my comb in here," I said. "I look like something left over from a shipwreck."

Teena joined me at the mirror. "That's about what we are," she said. "It's like we're stranded on an island. Nobody can get to us, and we can't get off."

"Don't talk like that!" I said.

"This big old house," she said. "I've never seen anything this huge and sprawled out. It would be easy for someone else to be in here with us, and we'd never know it."

"Don't do that, Teena!" I snapped. "We could scare ourselves into a panic."

She looked at me, and her eyes were wide and serious. "I'm just about there."

I turned and looked at her. "I feel the same way. I wish I could jump up and down and cry and scream for my parents, and they'd come and take me out of here."

Teena smiled. "Me, too. It's funny the things you think about when you're scared. I've been wishing I had the scrap of blanket I used to carry around when I was little."

"Good old security blanket," I said. "I had one, too."

"Yeah?" She cocked her head and studied me.

"I guess I've still got a kind of security blanket," I said. "It's tapioca pudding. I don't know why—maybe because Mom used to make it when any of us was getting over the measles and stuff like that—but tapioca pudding to me is one of the most comforting things in the world."

"If that's what you call it, then I've got one too. Mine's vanilla ice cream with chocolate syrup on it," Teena said, and we both laughed.

I opened the bathroom door and pulled her with me. "Come on. Let's get back to Bo and Julian. They'll wonder why we're taking so long."

But as we entered the hallway I stopped. "There's someone in the kitchen!"

"I heard it, too," she whispered.

"Whoever it is isn't trying to be quiet."

"You think it's Bo and Julian?"

"We can find out."

I led the way as we stepped very carefully along the hallway until we could see into the kitchen. Julian was opening cabinets and looking inside.

Teena and I gave such sighs of relief that they came out explosive with laughter.

Julian whirled. "Oh, it's you!"

"What are you doing?" I asked him.

"Bo sent me to find something for us to eat. He's keeping an eye on the television, in case there are any more weather warnings we should know about."

Teena and I crossed the large room. "Did you look in the refrigerator?" asked.

"Not yet," he said. "I feel like a burglar, helping myself to someone else's food."

I opened the refrigerator door and became suddenly hungry when I saw the wealth of apples and cheese and a loaf of bread. I pulled out a carton of milk, opened it, and sniffed. "The milk's good."

Teena and Julian looked over my shoulder. Julian examined a block of cheese with its foil wrapping wadded over the cut end, and peeled back the foil. "Anyone want a cheese sandwich?" he asked.

I took out the loaf of bread and handed it to him.

A large freezer stood next to the refrigerator, and Teena pulled it open. "There's plenty of food in here," she said. "This thing is stuffed."

I shut the refrigerator door. I didn't know how the others felt, but I was uncomfortable with my back to the room, so I leaned against the counter. The outside door shuddered against the gusts of rain and wind. It looked as though it would fly open at any minute, shattering the chair that propped it shut.

"We don't know for sure that Mrs. Gracie Ella didn't come back from Dallas," I said.

"So then, where is she?" Teena asked.

"Sooner or later we're going to have to look in that last room," I said.

"No!" Julian turned away from the counter and put a hand on my arm. "There's no point in going back there. As soon as the storm is over we'll turn the problem over to the police. They can handle it. There's nothing we can do."

I wasn't hungry any longer. "What's the matter with us?" I said. "Bo said we should all stick together, and we aren't doing it."

"Don't you want something to eat?" Julian asked.

"I suppose so," I said, "but let's get Bo in here, too." I hurried across the kitchen and ran down the hallway, the others right behind me.

As I entered the living room I could see the back of Bo's head resting against the flowered armchair. But in the chair next to his, also facing the dark television screen, was the back of another head!

I heard Teena gasp, and I grabbed Julian's hand. The fear inside me was so strong that the room seemed to fade in and out, and the stale odor of dying roses was suffocating.

None of us spoke. We just slowly walked toward the chairs. I wasn't conscious of moving my legs, but there I was, standing in front of the chairs, staring at a painted head that was propped up on pillows. Its glittering glass eyes seemed to stare back at me.

Teena shrieked. I opened my mouth, but was too frightened to make a sound. I could hear Julian saying, "Bo! Wake up!"

"Huh?" Bo's eyes slowly opened, and he rubbed them. "Oh," he mumbled. "I guess I fell asleep."

"How could you sleep?" Teena yelled at him.

Bo sat up, and for the first time saw what

was in the other chair. He staggered to his feet, stumbling backward, almost falling. "What's that? What are y'all doing?"

"We didn't do it," I told him.

Julian stepped forward and picked up the head. "It's made of some kind of plaster," he said. He held it toward me. "Is this anything a magician would use?"

I didn't want to touch it, but I took it from Julian. The glossy paint was cold, and those glass eyes seemed to be looking at me. The head was hollow and surprisingly light in weight. "I don't know," I said. "Magicians are showmen, and they try to make their acts unusual. There's no reason why a magician couldn't use this."

"It's gruesome!" Teena said.

"But people want to see gruesome things," I told her. "That's why there are so many tricks about people being sawed in half or having swords stuck through them. The audience knows it's an illusion, but still likes to think it's real."

"I don't want to talk about it," Teena said.

"What we need to talk about is who put the head here," Julian said. "And why."

"The 'why' is obvious," I said. "Someone wanted to frighten us."

"He did okay in that department," Teena said.

"Why'd you say 'he'?" I asked.

Teena just shrugged, but Bo said, "I shouldn't have gone to sleep. I can't do anything right."

"Don't say that, Bo," I told him. "We're all tired. If I'd been sitting there by myself, I probably would have gone to sleep, too."

Teena tossed the pillows out of the chair and flopped into it. She glared at me. "You know you're always saying something to try to make people feel better, Lisa. Always trying to be the good little girl. You're saying, 'See how sweet and nice I am.' What Bo did was dumb. He knows that. We know that. Cut the act."

"It's not an act!" I was so startled I couldn't think of anything else to say. It didn't matter, because Teena was wound up.

"How come you turned off the TV, Bo?" she demanded. "You were supposed to be watching for weather warnings."

"I didn't turn it off," he said. "I thought y'all did."

"This isn't getting us anywhere," Julian said. "There's no point in being angry. We're in this together."

"In what?" Teena snapped. "I'd like to know what we're fighting here. Up until now I've known my enemies and I either leave 'em alone or face up to them, but now I don't know where I stand."

"At least stop fighting us," I said. "We're not your enemies, Teena."

"Yeah? You're going to tell me that we're friends?"

I carefully placed the plaster head on a nearby end table. I sat in the chair next to Teena and motioned to Bo and Julian. "Let's talk," I said. "Sit down, and let's try to work out what we should do. We can't go on bickering. We've got to have some sort of plan."

Julian sank to the floor as a dancer would, curling into a cross-legged position. Bo came down heavily, awkwardly, squirming until his long legs were tucked in place.

"Julian had a good question," I said. "Who's in this house with us? We think the hitchhiker broke in, but both Black Beard and the woman said something about his no longer being here."

"And we know the woman who lives here is away," Julian said.

"Unless she did come back from Dallas," I added.

"But she's an old lady," Bo said. "She wouldn't do something like this."

"So?" Teena said, and her words came out with giggles. "You think all old ladies are nice? You need to meet some mean old lady like the one who lives on our street to find out what life's really all about."

"Maybe this Mrs. Gracie Ella came home and just didn't tell her friend down the road," Julian said. "She may be afraid of us and wish we'd leave, so she's trying to scare us away."

"It's possible," I said.

"So you think that's all it is, an old lady?" Bo asked.

Teena spoke up. "I don't see how it could be. If Mrs. Gracie Ella were here, don't you think she would have come out when her friend from down the road came by?"

"Good point," Julian said.

"There's one other possibility," Teena added. "We could be talking about a ghost."

We all stared at her. "Come off it," Bo said.

"A ghost wouldn't have put that head in the chair and turned off the television set."

"A poltergeist might," Teena said. "I've read about them. They play all kinds of tricks."

"A head propped up on cushions? It wasn't that big a deal."

"How about what scared Sam? How about what he saw in that back room?"

We thought about that for a moment. I didn't have an answer, so I was glad when Bo said, "The old lady probably pulled a gun on him. He might have thought she was going to shoot."

"No," Julian answered. "He was so frightened he passed out. Someone with a gun wouldn't have had that effect on him."

"Okay, doctor, tell us what would," Bo said.

Julian ignored the sarcasm in Bo's voice and answered, "Something Sam couldn't handle."

"You're making things too complicated," Bo said.

"You can't always search for a simple answer," Julian told him.

Bo lifted his hands as though there was something he wanted to say, but he just shook his head, looking completely bewildered.

"Maybe it is a simple answer," I said.

"Maybe what Sam saw was an illusion—something put there to frighten him."

"The kind of illusion a magician would create?" Julian asked.

"Maybe."

"But Mrs. Gracie Ella isn't a magician. It was her husband," Teena said.

A crack of lightning came so close I could hear it sizzle. I closed my eyes, clutching the arms of my chair. "I hate it!" I cried.

We waited for the crash of thunder, which roared and vibrated through the house like an angry spirit.

Even the silence that followed seemed to tremble. I could practically hear my father laughing and saying, "Lisa, you're a big girl. Surely you're not afraid of thunder and lightning! Why, that's only nature at work. Now, let's not hear any more of this foolishness about being afraid."

There was a long pause before I was able to say, "Do you think we should look for the person who is here and try to make our peace with her?"

"Look for her down that hallway?" Teena asked. "No way."

"We've got to do something," I said.

"Why don't we just stay here?" Bo asked. He added quietly, "And this time stick together."

Julian reached over and took both of my hands. "Listen to us, Lisa," he began.

The flash of lightning and thunder came almost as one, cracking and pounding and plunging us into darkness.

[SIX]

WE ALL began talking at once as we jumped to our feet. "The candles! Where are those candles?"

"Mrs. Whitt said—"

"Why didn't somebody—?"

"Look out, Bo! You're pushing me!"

"I'm trying to get to the sideboard."

"I can't see a thing!"

"Bo!"

A sudden thin stream of light beamed from Julian's fingers—a small flashlight attached to a key chain.

"That's not much good," Bo said.

"Shut up, Bo!" Teena snapped. "It'll help us find the candles."

We moved together to the sideboard. I shivered, and at the same time could smell the sour, damp fear in my body. Bo pulled the large center drawer open, and we all grabbed for the candles piled at one end.

"Who's got a match?" I asked.

"No sweat," Bo said. "There's some match folders right here."

No one spoke while we held our candles out for Bo to light. The walls of the room withdrew from us. We were marooned in little patches of ragged light.

Teena broke the silence, asking, "What do we do now? Walk around with these things like we're in some kind of procession?"

"There must be some candleholders around here," Julian told her.

"We can get the candle bottoms soft and stick them on saucers," I said.

"Saucers are going to be way back there in the kitchen." Teena's eyes widened as she spoke.

I automatically looked into the large drawer again, and what I saw was so exciting I shoved my candle at Julian, saying, "Hold this for me! Look what I've found!"

"Candleholders?" Teena asked.

"No," I said. I pulled out an armload of loose photographs and sheets of newspapers and put them on the top of the sideboard. Under them was a thick scrapbook, and I glanced inside. "This is terrific! Look! Photographs! Clippings! Even old playbills. Hey! Great Chamberlain performances!"

Teena reached into the drawer, coming up with a tidy packet of envelopes. They were tied tightly in the middle with a string. She handed them to me. "Want these, too?"

"Don't bother about that stuff now." Bo took the letters out of my hand, dropped them on the sideboard with the other things, and shoved the drawer shut. "We've got to find some candleholders and get more of the candles lit."

"Yeah," Teena said. "The more light in this place the better."

"Look in the dining room," I said. "That's where most people keep candleholders."

"Come on then," Teena said.

"You go," I said. "It isn't going to take four of us to walk into the next room. I want to look at this."

"We can't leave you alone!"

"I'll stay with Lisa," Julian said. "I'd like to see what she's found."

Bo grumbled something, but he and Teena went into the dining room, the light from their candles licking up and down the wall.

"Move your candle closer," I told Julian. I held up a black-and-white glossy photograph of a man dressed in evening clothes with a top hat and cape. "This must be Chamberlain the Great," I added.

"Look at that outfit," Julian said. "It's wonderful. Really the way a magician ought to look."

I pulled another photograph from the pile. "Here's a close-up of his face. He was a very handsome man."

"I wonder if he was a good magician." Julian took the photo from me and studied it. "I bet he liked being a performer, standing in that spotlight, and knowing he was giving something to his audience and they were enjoying what he was giving."

"I wish I could do it," I said.

Julian was quiet and I turned to look at him. The candlelight highlighted his high cheekbones and softened the shadows under his eyes. In a way it surprised me that Julian was handsome, too. I wondered why I hadn't noticed.

"Maybe a performer forgets the audience," he said. "There's something so absorbing about—well, about dancing, for instance—that the body movement, the feeling of being an extension of the music—" He stopped.

"Tell me," I said. "I've never thought about what it must be like to be a dancer."

"My parents like the theater and the ballet," he said. "We go to Dallas and to Houston, and even once in a while to New York for performances. When I was just a little kid I could feel that music move through my body like blood, and in my mind I was onstage, dancing, too."

"Was that when you began taking ballet lessons?"

He nodded. "I put up a bar in a room off the garage a few years ago, and I'd rather work out there than do anything else."

"Are you good?"

He looked at me suspiciously, and I said, "I mean it. You ought to be able to tell if you've got what it takes to be a professional dancer someday."

Julian took a long breath and looked so unhappy I was sorry I'd pried into his feelings. "My grandfather was a doctor. My father is a doctor. It's a family tradition," he said, and I could hear the bitterness in his voice.

"Service to the community plus an income good enough to provide for the finer things in life. Should be all I could want. Right? Much better than being a dancer and starving while I try to make it."

"I understand," I told him. I looked down at the photographs I had temporarily forgotten. "At least, I think I do."

I put the photographs on the sideboard and picked up a clipping. "There are so many worlds, and we've only got passes to a few of them."

Julian leaned close to read over my shoulder. His head touched mine, and for a moment I rested against him, enjoying the intimacy.

But Bo and Teena came into the room, surrounded with shaking fingers of yellow light. "Hey! Look what we found!" Teena said. "A candelabra!"

Julian and I moved apart.

"And there's a bunch of candleholders," Bo added. "Let's fill them up."

"We'd better not use all the candles at once," Julian said. "We don't know how long this storm will last, but I do know the electricity won't be back on until after it's over."

"Y'all haven't been noticing what's happening out there," Bo said. "That thunder and lightning moved off to the east after the big one hit."

As though to prove his point, there was a low growl of thunder in the distance.

"But the rain's still coming down hard," Teena said. She stepped forward. "What did you find in all that stuff, Lisa?"

"Some photographs of someone who I think must have been Chamberlain the Great." I handed them to her.

"That clipping tells about one of his performances," Julian said. "The reviewer liked the show."

"Look," I said. "Chicago in 1950. Before the Korean War."

"That Mrs. Gracie Ella must be ancient," Teena said.

I had picked up another glossy black-and-white photograph. "Here's a picture of Chamberlain with his assistant." I studied the small woman with the short blond hair and the heart-shaped face that looked back at me from the stiff, shiny photograph. "I wonder if his wife was his assistant."

"Does it give her name?" Julian asked. He leaned over my shoulder to peer at the paper. We were physically close again, but it wasn't the same.

"No," I said, "but she probably would have had a stage name anyway. For that matter Chamberlain the Great could have been named John Jones. Magicians usually want dramatic-sounding names."

"How about you, Lisa?" Teena asked. "If you were a real magician on a stage, would you have a different name?"

My face grew hot, and I was glad no one could see me blush. "When I was young and putting on my magic acts, I used to call myself 'Shandra the Wonder Girl.'" I giggled. "That was when I thought Wonder Woman in the comic strip was the greatest and wished I were just like her."

"You and Wonder Woman!" Teena laughed. "There's a big difference."

Julian smiled at me. "I don't see much difference."

I smiled, too, as the feeling of a special closeness with him returned. The Julian and Lisa who had worked together in class without really noticing each other seemed like two entirely different people.

"You're crazy," Teena said. She walked to the chairs that faced the blank television screen. "Why don't we sit down here and just wait for that storm to be over and for morning to come?"

"Just sit and wait?" I asked.

"I feel safer here than anywhere else in this house," she said.

"She's got a good point," Bo said. "Myself, I'd sort of like to see what we could find to eat in the kitchen, but since we know someone else is in this house, maybe just sitting and waiting is the smartest thing to do."

"If the woman who lives here has been the one trying to scare us away, then I guess you're right," Julian said. "She might feel more at ease if we stay in one spot."

I thought longingly of the black room filled with the tools of Chamberlain's trade. "I'd love to see Chamberlain's equipment," I said. "This might be the only chance I'd get."

"If you want to go into that scary old black room, you're out of your skull," Teena said.

"I wouldn't hurt anything. None of us would. I wish Mrs. Gracie Ella could understand that." Impulsively I turned to face the bedroom hallway at the far end of the room and raised my voice. "Please! Whoever you are! We aren't here to bother you! We won't hurt any of your things!"

Julian grabbed my shoulders, shaking me. "Don't do that!"

"Why did you stop me?" I demanded. "Maybe the best thing we could do is make contact with her."

"If that's who you're talking to. Remember that something—or someone—frightened that man from the Auto Club. We don't know who we're dealing with."

"Or what." Teena's voice trembled. "Let's just get together over here and stay put. I'd feel a lot better about it."

I closed my eyes and tried to relax and get

the feeling of the house and the person in it. Again the strange sensation crept through me that there was someone back in that room, another mind trying to shield its thoughts from me, to hide in a shadowy world I couldn't reach.

"Come on, Lisa!" Teena's voice was demanding.

Why, I don't know, but I took the close-up photograph of Chamberlain the Great and his assistant and propped it up against the vase of dying roses, where its glossy surface shimmered in the flickering candlelight.

This time Bo took the flowered chair next to Teena's. Julian sat on the floor, and again I perched on the brick ledge in front of the fireplace. Bo had put the candelabra on the end of the sideboard, and two of the single candles were on the table next to him.

"How did Abraham Lincoln study by candlelight without ruining his eyes?" Teena asked.

Bo yawned. "I give up. How?"

"What do you mean, 'how'? I don't have an answer."

"I thought you were telling a joke."

Teena snorted, and I said, "Maybe we should tell jokes. It might help."

"Now?"

"Why not? It will get our minds off—well—everything."

"Okay. That idea's better than nothing." Teena shrugged. "So who'll tell the first joke?"

"I'll be first," Bo said. He looked at Teena and me. "Ladies present, so that kind of limits things." He launched into such a dumb joke about a purple elephant that we all laughed.

"We heard that one in third grade!" Teena said.

But Bo looked pleased with himself. "So what? You laughed, didn't you? Let's hear your joke and see if it's so great."

"I wish you hadn't done that. Every time someone asks me to tell a joke they all go out of my head," Teena complained.

So Julian said, "My turn, then. How many politicians does it take to change a lightbulb?"

"How many?" I asked.

"Four," he said. "One to set up a fact-finding committee on the subject, one to take a tour of Europe to see how lightbulbs are changed in other countries, one to poll his constituents, and one to change it—four years later."

Teena and I giggled, but Bo's eyebrows came down in a wrinkled V, and he said, "I don't get the part about four years later. Are you making fun of Democrats or Republicans, and if they're already in office, why would it be four years?"

"You sure know how to ruin a joke," Teena grumbled. She sighed and leaned back in her chair.

Everyone was getting out of the mood fast. I hadn't taken my turn yet, so I made a desperate try to sound lighthearted and said, "Knock, knock."

A low whisper came back: "Who's there?"

Teena shrieked. "Bo! Stop that!"

"I didn't—" he began, but I shouted at him.

"We were trying to keep from getting scared, you nerd! Now you've ruined everything!"

"We know where the whisper came from," Julian said, and we all began shouting at Bo at once.

Finally Bo lifted both palms toward us, fingers outspread. "Shut up," he said. "Y'all aren't being reasonable, and no one's going to admit anything. So just shut up."

No one said anything. Maybe Julian and Teena felt as I did: pretty sure that the whisper was Bo's stupid idea of being funny, yet slightly suspicious of the others.

The rain made such a steady rhythm that it was almost hypnotizing, and I wished I could go to sleep. Like a kid, I wished for my own bed and my mother's hands tucking the covers around my chin, and her smile. *Mama,* I thought, *I wish I were home.* I leaned back against the rough brick and closed my eyes.

I wish I were a little girl, too young to worry about what's in this house. I don't want to get all tied up in knots about not doing well at the speech tournament, and grades, and trying to follow all the great things the rest of the family does. I pictured myself back in my room, with the old, flowered blue wallpaper and the Raggedy Ann doll tucked into my arms. Everything was so much simpler then, so comfortable, so uncomplicated.

"Cut it out, Lisa," Bo said. "That tapping's driving me nuts."

It dawned on me that I'd been hearing

tapping also. It just hadn't interfered with the warm, secure place to which I'd retreated. "I'm not tapping," I said.

"Then who—?"

We all sat upright. I scrambled to my feet. The tapping was coming from a spot above my head.

Teena's hands were over her mouth as she stared at the high mantel that crossed the fireplace about halfway up the wall. Bo and Julian stood like sculptures, their eyes wide and unblinking as they stared, too.

I whirled and saw a cluttered array consisting of a low vase of pussy-willow stems, a china cup and plate, some small pewter statuettes, and a wooden music box. Tucked among them, lying on the mantel, was a hand—a white, disembodied hand that vibrated in rhythm—tapping, tapping.

I don't know which shook me most, the initial shock of seeing the hand or the wave of relief I felt when I knew exactly what I was looking at.

I reached up toward the mantel, having to stand on the ledge to do so. The hand was smooth and cold, and I shuddered as I touched it, even though I knew what it was. Bo let out a rasping, animal-like noise as I picked up the hand and the metal plate under it, and jumped down with them.

Teena stared through her fingers, and Julian whispered, "What is it?"

"A wax hand," I said.

I turned it over so they could see the attached wires, and they came forward.

"What made it move?" Bo asked. He cleared his throat a couple of times, trying to bring his voice back to normal.

"See? Right here," I said. "There's a steel ball under the fingertips that hits the metal plate and makes the tapping sound. The wires are connected to a small battery."

"What's it for?"

"Scary stuff," I said. "A magician can make a hand tap on a table across the stage. It distracts people in the audience, too. While they're looking at the hand, he can do something he doesn't want them to notice." I paused. "These hands can be used in other ways, too."

"What other ways?" Julian asked.

"Séances," I said. "A lot of fake mediums use the hand to tap out 'yes' and 'no' signals.

You know—answers from the grave, that sort of thing."

Teena shuddered. "Why is it here?"

"I don't know," I said. "It's probably been here all this time, and we just didn't notice it. That mantel is pretty high. I didn't pay much attention to what was up there with all that stuff, did you?"

"Why did it suddenly start tapping?" Julian asked.

"It didn't start itself," I told him.

"No one was in here except us," he said.

"No one we could see," I answered.

Teena grabbed my shoulders and shook me, at the same time keeping away from the wax hand I was holding. "There you go again!" she cried. "You're making it worse, Lisa!"

I stepped back and studied the wax hand. They waited, looking at me.

"I don't mean to frighten anyone," I said. "And I don't know how this hand was set in motion, unless there's some mechanism up there on the mantel that's tied into a switch in another room. But I think I know why it was set to tapping."

"Why?" Julian asked.

"I think the person who tried to frighten us before had a reason for doing it again. She wants us out of this room."

"You mean she wants us out of this house."

I shrugged. "Probably. Unless it's this particular room."

"Maybe we should hole up in the kitchen," Bo said. He looked almost hopeful, and I wondered if he were thinking of food.

"No!" Teena said. "We'll have to go past that horrible magic room, and Lisa will want to go inside!" She scowled at me. "Put down that awful hand, and everybody sit down!"

As I put the hand on the table a rustling sound came from near the entrance to the dark hall.

We whirled to face a glowing ball that trailed gauzy wisps. This small spirit hovered in the blackness, dipping and trembling, then slowly moved toward us.

[SEVEN]

JULIAN QUICKLY stepped in front of me. "Go back!" he said.

I couldn't tell whether he was talking to the floating ball or to me.

Bo was at his side. Each word came out as slowly and heavily as poured molasses. "I'm not going to let that thing get to us."

I tried to shake off Teena's grip on my arm. "It won't hurt us," I said.

The glowing ball bobbed up and down, making short feints toward us, then retreating.

"It's not human," Teena whispered.

"It's only a lighted ball and some gauze," I said. "It's moved around by long tongs that can be opened out or folded in. They're called 'lazy tongs,' and most magicians use them for some kind of trick."

"Why don't we see the tongs?" Bo asked.

"Probably because they're black," I said. "Black on black usually can't be seen."

Teena nudged me. "Is that why we can't see the person who's doing the trick? Is he covered with black?"

I stepped forward, around Julian, and the ball retreated. "We don't know who you are," I called out. "But don't be afraid of us."

The ball moved back, forward a bit, then back, heading toward the bedroom hallway.

"What do you want?" I asked.

The ball was now in the archway, hovering, waiting.

"I think someone wants us to follow that thing," Julian said.

The ball immediately disappeared into the darkness of the hall.

"Not on your life!" Teena said. "Not down that hallway."

"Whoever is in this house is a magician," Julian said.

"Those are just basic magic tricks," I told him. "Almost anyone could do them."

"Like Mrs. Gracie Ella?"

"She must have seen her husband perform the tricks a million times. There's no reason why she couldn't do them. And if she used to be a medium, she probably used them to convince her clients she was communicating with the dead."

"I think we're dealing with a loony," Bo said. "How come the person doesn't talk to us? How come he wants to scare us? It doesn't make sense."

"Maybe we'll find out what this is all about if we do follow it into the hallway," Julian said. "If it's just someone doing magic tricks, it couldn't be dangerous."

I moved so that I was touching Julian. Somehow I felt more secure with the warmth of his body against mine. "A part of me keeps saying that we should investigate that back room, but another part keeps warning me to stay away. I don't know how the rest of you feel, but I don't think we should go into that hallway."

"I don't want any part of anything in this place!" Teena said. "And that hallway and whatever is in that back room are first on my list of things to stay away from!"

"Why don't we just go in the kitchen?" Bo said. "I'd feel better about staying there." When no one answered he added, "And we could get something to eat."

"The kitchen would probably be a good place," Julian said. "I don't think our invisible person wants us to stay in this room."

Teena was already reaching for the candelabra. "Take all the candles," she said, "and the matches."

I swept up the scrapbook with the pictures and clippings that were on it, but the packet of letters slid from my grasp. I tried to balance my armful of things while I stopped to get the letters, but Bo got to them first.

"I'll get it," he said, and he tucked the letters into his back hip pocket. "You're going to drop that whole mess of stuff if you aren't careful."

"What are you going to do with those, Lisa?" Teena asked.

"Read them," I said. "I want to find out more about Mrs. Gracie Ella and her magician husband."

We were almost at the entrance to the dining room, walking slowly in a tight pack, watching the candles to make sure they didn't flicker out, when I stopped. "Wait," I said. "Let's take our cases with us."

I glanced toward the front door, where our cases were still piled in a heap.

"Why?" Bo asked. "What good could they do us?"

"I don't know," I said. "It's just a feeling."

"Your feelings are creepy," Teena said, but Julian handed me his candle, crossed the room, and managed to juggle the four cases.

"Thanks," I said.

He smiled. "I believe in following hunches," he said.

"Even if they're somebody else's?" Teena asked.

"Especially if they're Lisa's," he answered.

I took one of the cases from Julian, and we re-formed our strange procession, trailing the wavering yellow light into the big kitchen.

Everything looked the same. There was a puddle of rainwater on the linoleum around the back door, but the chair was still holding the door fast.

"The wind is down," Julian said. He put the cases against the wall, and I put mine with them. I carried the pile of clippings and pictures to the table and stacked them at one end.

"What time is it?" Teena asked. "I think my watch stopped. It's got to be after midnight."

Bo placed the candelabra in the center of the table and looked at his watch. "One thirty," he said. "No wonder y'all are all so hungry. It's been a long time since lunch."

"If we're going to eat some of Mrs. Gracie Ella's food, we can leave some money on the kitchen counter," I said. "Whatever we think the food would have cost. That way we won't just be taking it."

"Right," Bo said. "I wouldn't want her to get mad at us."

"When she comes home and finds some food gone," Julian added.

"You don't think she's here?" I asked him.

"You're the one with the weird feelings," Teena told me. "You tell us who's in this house with us."

I pulled a wooden slat-backed chair away from the table and sank into it. "I'm tired," I said, ignoring Teena's statement. "All I want to think about is going home."

Bo opened the refrigerator. "Who wants a sandwich?"

"All of us," Julian said. "I'll help make them."

"I hate to cook," Teena said, sitting in the chair next to mine.

"Doesn't your old man do the cooking at home, too?" Bo asked her.

"He hates to cook," she said. "Since he's got to do it at the café, he won't go near the kitchen at home. I'm the one who makes most of the meals."

"It's probably good practice for you," Bo said. "Girls are supposed to be good cooks."

Teena slapped her hand on the table. "What a dumb thing to say! I suppose it's because we're all supposed to grow up to be good wives and mothers!"

Bo turned and stared at Teena, looking bewildered. A blob of mayonnaise dropped from the knife he was holding onto his hand, but he didn't seem to notice. "What's wrong with being a good wife and mother?"

"You and your little world of rednecks," she snapped. "You never change. It's the men who own the—"

I reached out to put a hand on her shoulder.

"Stop arguing! It's wasting a lot of energy! And we may need all we can get!"

"Why?" Teena stared at me.

Julian carried a plate of sandwiches and set it carefully in the middle of the table. "Because we'll have to stay awake," he said.

Teena looked toward the battered back door. "Oh," she answered.

Julian kicked out a chair and sat in it. He held the plate of sandwiches toward me. "Salami," he said, "and some kind of yellow cheese. I put some mustard in there, too."

"Sounds awful," Teena muttered. She hunched over in her chair and stared at the sandwiches.

"I always put mustard in salami sandwiches," I told Julian, and for some crazy reason we grinned at each other.

Bo licked the mayonnaise from his hand and joined us at the table. He was the first one to reach for a sandwich, taking a monstrous bite from the middle. "Mustard?" he mumbled with his mouth full.

For a few moments no one spoke. We were all busy eating. Then Teena said, "Somebody say something. All I hear is rain coming down, and I keep listening for some noise in-side the house, too. It's driving me bananas."

"Think about something else," I said.

"How can I?"

"Okay. We'll talk about something else. Want to read through these clippings about Chamberlain the Great?"

"I wish you hadn't brought those things in here!" Teena said. "Let's not even think about him!"

"All right," I said. "Don't get excited. We'll change the subject."

No one said a word. We just looked at each other hopefully. Finally Bo said, "Want me to tell you about the eight-point buck I brought down last year with my first shot?"

"No!" Teena said. "I don't want to hear about hunting either! How can you justify killing a defenseless animal?"

Bo just looked at her. "For food."

"Food? You mean because you like to kill things."

"I mean for food, stupid. We dressed it and got the meat cut into steaks and chops and ground for sausage, and froze it, and we ate that meat during the next six months or so."

"Well," she said, "that deer was a beautiful animal in the forest before you killed it."

"Is that how you count what gets eaten or not—how beautiful it is? That why you can sit there and gobble up those salami sandwiches? Because the pig wasn't beautiful?"

"That's not what I mean," she said. "I just—well, I guess if you use the meat, hunting's okay. I just don't understand people who like to hunt."

Bo leaned back in his chair and wiped his shirtsleeve across his mouth. "Y'all don't want to understand," he said.

A gust of rain slapped against the side of the house, and the door creaked and shivered. Teena rested her elbows on the table and propped her chin in her hands. The edge was gone from her voice. "Tell us about yourself, Bo," she said. "We do want to understand."

"What's there to tell?" Bo asked. "I just live like everybody else."

Julian shook his head. "No. You're not like everyone else. None of us knows what it's like to be in your shoes."

"Yeah," Teena added. "Big football star, one of the popular people at school. Great big house and a daddy with a car agency and plenty of money."

I put a hand on Teena's arm. "You asked Bo to tell us about himself. Don't *you* tell *him*."

Bo brushed a strand of sun-bleached hair out of his eyes and scowled at Teena, so I added, "Bo, how does it feel to play football? Do you get real excited before the games? Is there a lot of pressure to win?"

He nodded. "Naw. I don't get excited. 'Pressure' is the word, I guess. Sometimes I even throw up before a game. All I know is I've got to go out there and look good. Each time I hope I don't do something dumb."

"Like fumbling the ball," Teena said.

"Why'd you have to bring that up?" Bo shifted in his chair, his feet hitting the floor with a bang. "You don't think I heard enough from my old man about that fumble in the last game?"

"I don't know what you're talking about," Teena said.

"The game with Hardy," he said. "Isn't that what you meant?"

Teena shook her head. "I didn't even see the game. I don't go to the football games."

Bo's eyes opened wide. "You don't? Why in hell not?"

"Because I work after school," Teena said.

"There's the night games," he said.

"Bo! There's more stuff to think about than football!" she answered. "Aren't you ever going to do anything else but play football?"

"Sure," he said. "Four years of football in college, then I come back to Clodine, and my old man will train me to someday run his dealership. And I guess I'll get married and have some kids."

Julian suddenly leaned forward. "Is that what you really want to do, Bo?"

"Why not?" Bo said. "What's wrong with it?"

"Nothing," Julian said. "If it's what you want."

"What's all this stuff about what I want? The plan makes sense, doesn't it? I play football. It gets me into college, and then I get out and work for my old man, and everybody's happy. Right?"

"Sounds to me like you're doing what your daddy and mama want," Teena said. "That is what your mama wants for you, too, isn't it?"

Bo shrugged. "I don't know what my mama

wants. Probably what my old man wants. She never said."

Teena got up and walked to the sink. She opened a cabinet and pulled out a glass. "We got something in common, Bo," she said. "We're both trying hard to do what our parents expect us to do."

"Amen," Julian murmured.

Teena turned and held the glass toward us. "Anybody want a drink of water?"

A sudden thud shook the back door. Teena dropped the glass, which shattered around her feet. As we waited, motionless, a scratching, scrabbling sound came from the other side of the door.

I jumped to my feet and clung to the back of the chair. "Something's out there," I whispered.

Bo was the first to react. He strode to the door and bent down to listen. "Can you hear it?" he asked. "Kind of a whining. Sounds like an animal."

"Open the door," Julian said. I found I was gripping his hand, awfully glad he was next to me.

Bo tugged the chair out from under the

doorknob, sliding it through the shiny puddle. With the chair still in his left hand like a weapon, he slowly opened the door. "How about that," he said, pushing the chair to one side and opening the door wider. "It's a black Lab. Looks half-drowned."

The dog wiggled through the door as Bo was speaking. It stood spraddle-legged in an aura of droplets as it shook itself again and again.

Bo slammed the door shut and wedged the chair back in place. Then he bent down to check the dog. "Where'd you come from, girl?" he asked. He looked up at us. "No tags on her collar, but she's been cared for." Bo gently stroked the dog's head and neck, and she turned and licked his hand. "Bet you're a good retriever, girl," he said, and the dog nuzzled against him.

I helped Teena pick up the countless shards of glass, while Julian gave the dog the rest of the salami and cheese. She gobbled them from his hands, licking his fingers afterward.

"Poor thing," I said. I went to the small window over the sink and tried to peer into the darkness. "It looks like everything's covered with water. It's a good thing the dog didn't drown."

"Water's almost up to the back steps," Bo said. "Whoever built this place knew enough about the floodplains to make sure the house would be high enough to stay dry."

I opened and closed kitchen drawers until I found a stack of dish towels. I whistled for the dog, and when she came I kneeled next to her and tried to rub her dry. "She smells as bad as that sweater I took off," I said as I tried to dry her before she wiggled away from my grip.

The dog backed off and shook herself again when I gave up, letting her go. I left the damp towels on the floor and got to my feet. "I wonder where she came from."

"Probably one of the places around here," Julian said. "She must have seen the light and known it probably meant people who could help her."

"I'm glad she came," Teena said. "I feel better having a big dog here to protect us."

"Me, too," I said, and we laughed.

Bo sat at the table again, and the dog laid

her head on his leg, her rear end whipping back and forth in joy.

"She really took to you," I said.

"Dogs are smart," he said. "They know who likes them."

Julian stretched and yawned. "What time is it now?" he asked.

Bo twisted his arm to look at his watch. "Just a couple of minutes after two."

"You're kidding!" I said. "It feels as though we've been in this room for hours!"

"Maybe your watch stopped," Teena said.

Bo held it to his ear and scrunched up his face to listen. "Still ticking," he said.

The rest of us wandered back to the table, taking the seats we had before, as though they'd been assigned. "Did you ever notice how people keep doing things the same way over and over again?" I asked. "We all took the chairs we had before."

"Big deal," Teena said. "What's that supposed to prove?"

"Nothing," I said. "It was just something I thought about."

"I wish we had some cards," Bo said. "We could at least be doing something."

"We could try some more jokes," I suggested, but Teena groaned, and Julian shook his head. "Okay," I added. "Not a good idea."

"Y'all asked me to tell you about myself," Bo said. "How about someone else taking a turn?"

"Okay. We can ask Julian why he has to be a doctor when he doesn't want to be," Teena said.

"Pass," Julian said. He stared down at the table.

"How come?" Bo asked. "A while ago y'all were putting the screws on me."

"I've got an idea," I said. "I'll do a magic trick."

"No, thanks!" Teena said. She shuddered.

"Just a simple coin trick," I said. "Nothing mysterious. Anyone have a quarter or a nickel on them?"

Julian reached into his jeans pocket and pulled out a couple of coins. "If the trick's any good you can keep them," he said.

I looked at the quarters in my hand. "I'll never get rich this way."

"At least you're not working for peanuts."

I laughed and put one of the quarters off to the side. "All right. Everyone put your hands on the table in front of you. Straight out, like mine."

They did, and Bo asked, "Where's the quarter you were holding in your right hand?" He looked at Julian and Teena with a satisfied smile. "I was keeping an eye on her."

I turned my right hand palm upward. "What quarter?" I asked. I turned up my left hand. "Do you mean this one?"

"I guess I wasn't paying attention while you did that," Bo said. "Try it again."

So I placed the quarter on the table and carefully put my right hand over it. "Were you watching carefully?" I asked him.

"I sure was. We all saw you put it under your right hand." He grinned. "Ruined the trick, didn't I?"

"Not really," I answered. I turned my right hand up. The quarter had disappeared.

"Okay," Bo said. "Left hand then. How'd you do it?"

I turned my left hand up. No quarter.

"I think you took my quarter," I told him, reaching over to pull it from behind his ear.

"Show us how you do that," Teena said.

"Nope," I said. "Magicians are very careful

to keep their tricks secret. If everyone knew how to do them, it would be the end of the game."

"A game?" Julian asked. "But some people do it for a living."

"They're lucky," I told him.

"Is that how all magicians feel about what they do—that it's a game?" Teena asked.

"I'm not making light of it," I told them. "Performing magic can be extremely dangerous. Did you ever hear of Houdini? He did all sorts of tricks that could have killed him if he hadn't been expert in what he was doing."

"Could magicians ever kill anyone else?" Teena asked. "Like an assistant—someone who's helping them?"

I thought a moment. "Maybe."

"Houdini," Julian said. "I read about him in a magazine article a year or so ago. Isn't he the one who promised he would make contact with his wife after he was dead?"

"Yes, but he—"

I didn't finish because Bo suddenly shoved his chair back. "Where's the dog?"

We all jumped to our feet, looking around the kitchen.

"Lisa!" Teena said. "Did you—?"

"Of course not," I told her. I looked toward the open doorway leading into the hall. "The dog probably went in there."

We looked at each other. "She didn't bark," Julian said. "I think she would have if she discovered someone else in the house."

"She didn't bark at us," I said.

Bo stepped to the doorway. "I'll call her," he said, and he proceeded to shout and whistle.

We waited, but she didn't come back. In all that darkness there was only silence.

"A big black dog disappears just as strangely as it appears," Teena murmured. "What do we make of that?"

None of us had an answer.

[EIGHT]

"WAS THAT dog for real?" Teena asked.

"Of course it was," I said. I brushed my hands down the front of my blouse, which was still damp from my attempt to dry the animal.

"I've read stories about ghost dogs," Teena said. Her chin jutted out stubbornly as she thrust her face up toward Bo's. "Don't laugh at me! There are such things as ghost dogs!"

"I'm not laughing," Bo said. "There's nothing funny about that dog's disappearing the way she did."

Julian was still staring into the darkness beyond the kitchen. "Magicians can make things disappear."

"An illusion," I said.

"Do you know how they do it?" Teena asked.

"Yes."

"How?"

Before I could answer, Bo said, "I better go after that dog."

I put a hand on his arm. "You can't do that."

He frowned at me. "We can't let something happen to her."

"We can't let something happen to you."

"Lisa's right," Julian said. "Remember? We decided to stick together."

Bo's laugh had no humor in it. "Then y'all better stick with me while I find the john."

"In that case," Teena said, "togetherness isn't the answer."

"I'll go with you," Julian said. "Lisa and Teena can wait here in the kitchen."

"And then we'll see about the dog," Bo said. He went to the table and picked up one of the candleholders, jerking it out of the puddle of hardened wax that had spilled over the edge. His eyes narrowed for a moment, and I wondered what he was thinking. "I better take another for Julian," he said, reaching for a second candle.

"Those candles are getting a lot smaller," Teena said. "We're going to have to light some others soon."

Julian took my hand, and his fingers were strong and warm. "You and Teena sit where you were," he told me, "where you can see the doorway. If you're at all nervous about anything, yell, and we'll come in a minute."

"All right," I said.

He squeezed my hand. "You'll be okay." It was both reassurance and a question, but I was getting another message, too. I knew it was important to Julian that I would be safe while he was away.

I watched him leave the room, his long, slender body moving easily, and I wanted to follow him, to touch him. At that moment, more than anything else in the world, I wanted Julian to hold me. I had never felt like this about any boy. My whole body was responding to him, and the intensity of my feelings frightened me.

"I hate this place!" Teena said. Her words snapped me to reality.

We walked back to our chairs at the table. The room had a musty odor I hadn't noticed before. It was a decaying, mildewy smell as though the walls themselves were damp.

"When is this rain going to stop?" In frustration I slapped the tabletop.

"No use beating on the furniture," Teena said. She cocked her head and appraised me. "Although maybe it's a good thing for you to do."

"No, it isn't," I said, rubbing my hand. "That stung."

"I mean, it's the first time I've seen you let loose enough to get mad."

I leaned back in my chair. "It never helps to get angry."

"Your mama teach you those words of wisdom?"

"What difference does it make?"

"Might make a lot of difference to you. You the first child, baby of the family, or what?"

"Baby!" I spit out the word. "I guess that's what I am, all right. The baby, trying to keep up with the others."

I stared at Teena, waiting to see how she'd react, but she just sat there as though she expected me to continue. "I've got an older brother and sister," I said. "They're both in law school."

When I paused, Teena said, "Both of them pretty smart, I guess."

"You guess right."

"Lots of honors and stuff like that all through school."

"Yes."

"How about you?"

I leaned into my hands, propping my elbows on the table. "Oh, Teena," I said, "I'll never catch up. I study all the time, and it doesn't come that easily."

"You get good grades, don't you?"

"I grind for them, and they aren't really that good. I'll make it into college, but without all those awards after my name on the graduation program."

"Your parents expect all that from you?"

"You know it."

She sighed. "Funny thing. We both got pressure on us to make good for two opposite reasons. No matter how you look at it, I guess we're stuck."

I nodded. The rain was still a steady tattoo

against the roof, but it seemed lighter, not as noisy as before. "Listen," I said. "Does it seem to you that the worst of the storm is over?"

She frowned, listening intently. "Maybe so. I don't think it's raining as hard as it was."

I reached over to the scrapbook and pulled it toward me.

"Why do you want to read that?" Teena made a face and shifted in her chair so that she was turned away from me.

"I want to find out more about the woman who lives here," I said. "Maybe something in this scrapbook will tell us.

"I just want to get out of here," Teena mumbled.

I began to read. There were short items from small town newspapers mostly. The Great Chamberlain usually rated only a few paragraphs, and many of the stories were written in the same style, as though some bored reporters copied their material from the Great Chamberlain's flyers.

I examined faded and yellowed newspaper photographs, many from the same glossy print that the magician must have sent to the newspaper as handouts. The pose was dramatic, the face handsome and arrogant. In an occasional photo the small blond woman appeared, a shy shadow beside—and slightly behind—the cape-swathed magician.

One of the photos made me feel creepy. It looked like an old-fashioned family pose, with the blond woman seated stiffly in a chair and Chamberlain standing behind her, one hand on her shoulder. On her lap, where a child might be, dressed in the clothes of a child, sat a ventriloquist's dummy with a humorless painted smile and glittering glass eyes that seemed to stare into the camera. Under the picture were her name and Chamberlain's, written in small cramped letters: Gladys and Harry Polowski, 1953.

"That's funny," I said.

"There's nothing funny about any of this."

"I mean strange funny. According to this, the Great Chamberlain's real name is Harry Polowski, and his wife's name is Gladys Polowski."

She looked up. "Another wife?"

"I don't think so."

"Gladys Polowski. Gracie Ella Porter. Same initials," Teena said.

"Why would she change her name?"

"Don't ask me. Why don't you put that stuff away?" Teena began humming to herself, a two- or three-note tuneless drone that began to drive me crazy, so I told her so.

"When are you going to get through with those things?" she countered.

"Teena, I've figured out some things about Chamberlain the Great, or Harry Polowski."

She moved an inch or two in her chair. At least now I didn't have to talk to her back. "Like what?" she asked.

"For one thing, he wasn't famous. Mostly he seemed to play small towns and just a few cities, and there aren't any really enthusiastic reviews in here."

"So what does that prove?"

I shrugged. "Look at this house. It's not the kind of house a second-rate entertainer could afford."

Teena twisted toward me, resting her arms on the table. "That Mrs. Whitt who was here— she said the house was bought with insurance money."

"He must have carried a lot of insurance."

"Did you find anything about the fire in that stuff you read?"

I looked at the clipping I had put on top of the pile. "I was just getting to it when you started making that noise."

Her mouth twisted in a grimace. "I was humming."

"Well, don't for a while, and I'll read this."

She was silent as I scanned the article. When I looked up she said, "Well?"

"It doesn't add anything to what we know. It was an old theater in a small town in Ohio. Chamberlain had gone backstage to check out arrangements the day before he was to move his equipment in and put on a show."

"What kind of arrangements?" Teena interrupted.

"Oh, trapdoors, backdrops, things like that."

I opened my mouth to continue, but Teena said, "Wait a minute. You mean magicians use trapdoors?"

"Sometimes. More of the older magicians used them than those of today."

"That's cheating," she said, and she looked so indignant I giggled.

"I told you magic is an illusion," I said.

She sniffed. "Go on with the newspaper story."

"There isn't much more. Something backstage caught fire while he was there. Apparently there were only a few people in the place, watchman, deliverymen, and so forth. They all got out except Chamberlain. The old theater burned to the ground, and firemen found Chamberlain's body after the fire was put out. A stagehand tried to save Chamberlain's life they think. He was badly burned—on the critical list, the newspaper says."

"Did he die, too?"

"I can't find any more clippings about him. I don't know."

"How'd they know that the body they found was the magician's?"

"Don't ask me," I said. "I suppose from what he was wearing."

"That would have got burned up, too."

"There's always a watch, a ring, something to identify a body," I said. "And Chamberlain seems to have been the only one missing."

"And his wife got the insurance money."

"What's wrong with that?"

"Think about it," Teena said. "She lived in a lot better style than she did while she was married to him. And that Mrs. Whitt said he was a mean old devil. It all worked out nice for Mrs. Gracie Ella, didn't it?"

"We don't even know those people. You shouldn't think things like that."

"I can think anything I want to think."

Teena's suspicions made me so uncomfortable I didn't know how to answer her, and she apparently had nothing else to say to me. We just stared at each other.

A thought waggled into my mind, blotting out the Great Chamberlain. "Teena!" I said. "Julian and Bo have been gone for a long time! They should have been back by now!"

She didn't answer, but we both slowly pushed back our chairs and walked to the open doorway. A gust of cold air from the crack around the back door whipped around my shoulders, and I shivered.

"Do you hear anything?" I asked as we waited.

Teena shook her head. "What should we do?"

"Get a candle," I whispered. "We'd better look for them."

Teena took a step backward, and her voice quavered. "We can't, Lisa. It's like walking into a hole. It swallowed up the dog. It swallowed up Bo and Julian. Not us, too!"

Teena was right. The darkness was like a yawning mouth. I shuddered as I stared into it, but I didn't step back. On the contrary, I had a compulsion to fall into that blackness, and I put out a hand to cling to the door frame.

"Lisa!" Teena's voice was as sharp as a slap between the shoulder blades. "Come away from there!"

But the walls in the hallway were wavering, touched with a glow that shattered the darkness. Someone was walking toward me, carrying a candle that reflected in his eyes. As he came closer I could see that it was Julian. I realized that I hadn't been breathing, and I let out a long sigh.

"Don't be frightened," Julian said, but there was tension in his face, and his jaw muscles were pulled tight.

"What happened?" I asked him, following him to the kitchen table. "Where's Bo? Where have you been?"

"What's wrong?" Teena demanded.

"I don't know," Julian said. "It's because of the dog. Bo had to look for it, and he wouldn't wait for me."

"So where is he?" Teena asked.

"It's crazy!" Julian put his candle on the table and spread his arms wide. "I looked for him in the dining room and back in the living room. Nothing."

"Down that hallway to the bedrooms?" My voice came out as a whisper.

Julian just looked at me. "No," he finally said.

"Poor Julian. You got guilt all over your face like jam," Teena said. "We didn't expect you to go back there. If Bo was stupid enough to go alone to find that dog—"

The echo of what she had said hung in the silence, bouncing back and forth in my mind.

"We'll have to go after him," I said.

"I came back to tell you what happened," Julian said. "And to ask you to go with me. I think we should go together." His eyes were so beseeching I took his hand. "I'm not a coward," he added.

"If you went into that hallway by yourself you'd be a fool," I told him.

Teena wailed. "That stupid dog! Why'd she have to come here? Why'd Bo have to do such a dumb thing?"

"He was really worried about the dog," Julian said.

Teena flopped into the nearest chair. "I don't understand that redneck turkey. He goes out and kills animals and brags about it, and at the same time he does some fool thing to save another animal. What's with him?"

"This animal's a dog, and that's the difference," I said. "Don't you see?"

"I don't even care," Teena said.

"But you care enough about Bo to want to find him, don't you?"

She stared at the floor and said, "I'm mad! I'm mad at Bo for making us have to do it!"

I leaned on the table, shoving my face toward her and yelling, "Do you think you're the only one? I'm furious with him because his car broke down and he got us into this mess, and I'm angry because he thinks he's so macho he could just go off on his own. But we can't sit and pout about it! We've got to find him!"

I tried to brush away the tears on my

cheeks while Julian put an arm around my shoulders. "Lisa, please don't cry," he said.

For some reason this made me angrier than before, and I twisted away from him. "I always cry when I get angry! I've always done it, and it makes me even more angry, because I never win arguments, and my sister and brother laugh at me, and—" I broke off, rubbing at my eyes with the end of my shirt.

There was silence for a few moments. Then Teena asked quietly, "Are you okay now?"

I nodded. "I'm sorry. I shouldn't have exploded at you."

Teena shrugged. "Doesn't matter. At least you let me know how you felt." She got up and walked to me, putting a hand on my shoulder. "You know, I would have gone with you to look for Bo. I just wanted to gripe about it for a while. That's the way it is with me. You wouldn't understand that, because you hold it all in and try to be Miss Sweetness while you're doing something you don't want to do. I operate a different way."

She turned to Julian. "You and Lisa have got a lot in common. Looking at you is like staring at a window with the shade pulled down. There's no way to tell what you're thinking or feeling."

"It isn't important for people to know." Julian pointed to the table. "Get the candles. We'll look for Bo."

"I'll put some new candles in the holders," I said. "These have almost burned themselves away."

Teena helped me. "Shall we bring this big thing with us?" she asked, holding up the candelabra.

"Better leave it here," I said. I looked around the kitchen, wondering why a kitchen always seems to be the most comforting room in a house. "We'll want this room to be lighted when we come back to it."

"Ready?" Julian asked.

Teena stepped forward, but I shook my head. "Before we go out there we need to think about who else is in this house, who we're going to be up against."

"Who? Or what?" Teena mumbled.

We didn't move. We simply stared at each other.

[NINE]

"IF THERE were just something to let us know if Mrs. Gracie Ella had come back from Dallas," Julian said.

I gasped as a memory jolted my mind. "There is!" I said. "Remember, Teena? We looked into the garage, and there's a car parked in it!"

She frowned. "Are you sure?"

"I know I saw a car, because I was thinking how crowded the garage was."

"I don't remember," Teena said. "I don't think I looked in the garage. I remember wishing you'd stop poking around all those rooms."

"We can find out by taking another look," I said as I picked up a candle.

"Where is the garage?" Julian asked.

"There's a door to the garage across the hall. Come on."

I led the way, unwilling to look down the hall. Maybe I was afraid of what I might see. *Mrs. Gracie Ella, why are you doing this to us?* I wondered. What kind of a strange person must she be?

It was just a few steps down the hall to the door. I put my hand on the knob and tried to turn it. "That's funny. It's stuck," I said.

Julian's hand was on mine, and I slipped my fingers away as he gripped the knob. "It's not stuck. It's locked," he said.

"Why?" Teena asked.

"Someone doesn't want us to go into the garage," I said.

"Maybe Mrs. Gracie Ella's afraid that if we find her car we'll use it to drive away," Teena said.

"I don't think so," Julian said. "Not with the water so high. We couldn't drive anywhere."

"Then why would she lock the garage?"

Julian and I looked at each other, and I knew his thoughts were the same as mine.

"Because there's something else in the garage that she doesn't want us to see," I said.

"Like Bo?" The words were whispered, but they seemed to echo through the hallway.

"I think we'd better try to break the lock," I said.

Julian bent over to peer at it. "It's just one of those knobs they often put on inside doors. Has a hole in the center, and you can stick something in, wiggle it, move the tumbler, and open the lock."

"Have you got something that will fit?"

Julian pulled a small pocketknife from his back jeans pocket, opened a thin blade, and tried it in the hole. "Too wide," he said. He got to his feet. "Does either of you have a hairpin or something like that?"

"Girls haven't worn hairpins for centuries," Teena said. "There's got to be something in the kitchen. Maybe a skewer. I'll go back and look."

She hurried off, shielding her candle.

"Lisa," Julian said, "Teena was right about my not being able to show my feelings. It's hard for me, especially when I really like someone, when I'd like to be able to tell her how I feel, but—"

Teena's shriek was so terrifying I was paralyzed for a moment. Then I seemed to be running in slow motion, sheltering my candle with one hand to keep it from flickering out. Julian pushed through the door with me into the darkened room.

Teena's back was toward the kitchen sink, and she held a long skewer with its point up as though she were protecting herself.

"What happened?" Julian asked, and when she didn't answer he shouted, "Teena! Tell us what happened!"

"Are you all right?" I asked. I reached her and put an arm around her shoulders. "Why did you scream?"

She took a couple of quick breaths, panting like an animal, before she was able to speak. "Somebody was in here," she said. She waved the skewer toward the kitchen table. "Whoever it was took the candelabra."

"Did you see who it was?" Julian asked.

"No," Teena said. "I had just found this skewer in the third drawer down, and all of a sudden I realized the light from the candelabra was gone and somebody was behind me, reaching for my candle."

"Where was your candle?" I automatically looked around.

"It was on the counter," Teena said. She stooped and picked up the candle and candleholder, fitting them together again. Then she stared at the skewer. "All I saw was an arm, but the arm and the hand were covered with black. And it was just for a minute, because I grabbed for the candle and at the same time I turned and hit out with this thing."

"Did you—?" I couldn't finish the sentence.

"I scratched somebody," she said. "It was dark, and I don't know how bad I hurt her."

"Her?"

"I don't know what to call the person who was here. I just know that there was a real body in the room, not a ghost."

Julian reached out and ran his index finger over the end of the skewer. As he pulled his finger away we could see a dark smudge on it. He rubbed his finger down the side of his jeans. "You scratched the person enough to draw blood."

"Oh, gosh," Teena said, "I've never deliberately hurt anybody in my life." She began to tremble.

"It was probably just a scratch," I told her.

Her chin came up angrily. "How do you know?"

"I don't!" I snapped. "But what am I supposed to say? I was just trying to help you!"

"There you go again! There's no rule that says you have to try to help me. This is something I've got to handle myself."

I had the weird feeling of someone's mind reaching out to mine. It's the way you feel when you're reading in the library, begin to feel uncomfortable, and finally look up, and someone's watching you. I slowly looked around the room. "There must be another door in here, one we haven't seen."

Julian followed me across the big room and turned the knob on a door between two cabinets.

"That should be a closet," he said, but it wasn't. As he swung the door open we could see into the black room that held the magic props.

I began to get excited. "Earlier I saw a door

on the other side of that room that probably leads into the hallway. What if there's another door that goes into the first bedroom on that side of the other hall?"

"Then somebody could get around in this house without going down the hallways," Teena said, practically in my ear. "Why?"

"No special reason," I said, but Teena persisted.

"Maybe there's a reason a magician would know about. You tell us, Lisa. You're the one who knows about magic."

"A magician wouldn't need extra doors in the rooms of his house. They were probably put in for convenience by the person who had this house built."

"How about extra doors in the house of a medium who uses them to trick her customers? Mrs. Gracie Ella is a medium," Teena said.

"But she'd have to have an accomplice to help her with her séances, and from what Mrs. Whitt told us, I'd guess that those séances were simple, one-person productions."

"Lisa's right. The doors could have been

here when the woman bought the house," Julian said.

"It doesn't matter who's right," Teena answered. "What matters is that whoever is in this house has a lot of ways to get to us. There's probably other ways we don't even know about."

"I think we're trying to figure out too many things," I told them. "Why don't we get busy and see if we can get the door to the garage open?"

We retrieved Teena's candle, which she lit from mine, and left the kitchen. We moved together so closely it made me want to giggle in spite of my fear. Maybe it was *because* of my fear. I felt like Coke inside a bottle that had been shaken, with giant bubbles of laughter and shrieks and yells shooting up to the top, ready to explode if the cap came off.

When we reached the door, Teena automatically tried the knob. It resisted, so she handed me her candle, thrust the pointed end of the skewer into the doorknob, and jiggled it around.

"I think I got it," she said, turning the knob.

The door opened without a sound. She took her candle from me, and the three of us held our candles up and outward, trying to penetrate the darkness of the garage.

"The car *is* there," I said.

"So that means Mrs. Gracie Ella did come home, and she's the one who's trying to drive us crazy," Teena said.

At first I thought the movement was my imagination, or maybe I thought it was caused by the shimmering light from our candles. "Did you see—?" I began, but the words turned to rocks in my throat, and I coughed and gasped as a large, black shape slowly rose in the front seat of the car.

"It's the dog!" I heard Julian say.

The Labrador immediately began to whine and paw at the side window, begging us to let her out.

My foot was already on the steps leading down into the garage, when Julian grabbed my shoulder. "Wait a minute," he said. "Suppose all three of us rush over there to let the dog out of the car? What's to stop Mrs. Gracie Ella from locking us in the garage?"

I looked down the hallway. No one was in sight. "Do you think two of us should stay here and keep watch?"

"Yes," he said. "I'll get the dog."

"I like dogs," Teena told Julian. "You stay here, and I'll get her."

"No," Julian said. He was staring at the trunk of the car, and I felt his thoughts with an icy shiver down my backbone. Teena didn't understand. "The car may be locked," I told her. "Julian might have to force it open or break a window, or—"

Julian was already down the short flight of cement steps. He pushed a large packing box aside and put his hand on the car door. "It's unlocked," he said, but he didn't open the door.

"Well? Let the dog out then," Teena said.

Julian looked at me. "The keys are in the ignition."

I nodded. "Then you can use them to—"

"I will."

Teena stared from Julian to me. "What are you two talking about?"

Julian opened the door, and the dog bounded out, planting wet kisses on his hands and jumping against his legs. As Julian reached inside the car to get the keys, the dog ran to Teena and to me, nuzzling us with affection.

"She's glad to get out of there," Teena said.

"Hang on to her," I said. I watched Julian squeeze between the car and the garage door and insert the trunk key into the lock. As the lid of the trunk swung up I held my breath.

Julian slammed the lid down and shook his head. "Empty," he said. He looked as relieved as I felt.

Teena let go of the dog's collar, stood upright, and stared at me, her mouth dropping open. "You mean you thought Bo was in the trunk of that car?"

I shook my head, trying to shake away the fear the way the Lab had shaken off the raindrops that had clung to her coat. "It was just an idea," I said. "We had to start somewhere."

"That's creepy!" Teena said. "That means you think the old lady who lives here is more than just crazy. You think she's dangerous!"

Julian came up the stairs, and we closed the door to the garage, "Yes," I said. "I guess we do."

"What reason would she have for hurting Bo?"

"What reason has she had for all the things she's been doing?"

"Then we better try to find Bo, quick."

"I think the dog can help us," Julian said.

"She doesn't know Bo."

"But she'll be aware of other people in the house. Maybe she'll seek him out."

I looked down at the Lab, who was rubbing against Teena's jeans. "Come on, girl," I said. "Come with us and find Bo."

We looked in the butler's pantry first, checking all the cupboards. Many of them were empty, but a few held a set of china and some mismatched crystal.

"What if he's hurt?" Teena said.

"Don't think about it," Julian told her. "We'll look through the empty bedroom and bath next."

The dog bounded ahead of us as though she were playing a game, and she kept looking back questioningly, wondering what we had in mind, I guess. She still had that wet-dog smell that reminded me of the damp sweater I had left by the door. I wasn't cold, but I missed the warmth of that sweater. For some reason I'd have felt more secure if I had been bundled up. My take-it-with-me security blanket? Maybe so. How many security blankets did I have?

The service porch contained a washer and dryer speckled with rust from the humidity. But the room was spotless, the cans and bottles of soap and cleanser in a tidy row on the open shelf above the appliances.

As we shut the door to the service porch I said, "There's another room in this wing of the house that we haven't explored yet."

Teena shuddered. "That black room with the magic stuff. What makes you think Bo's in there?"

"We don't know where he is," I said. We had come down the hallway as far as the closed door to the black room. "We'll have to check all the rooms."

Teena put a hand on my arm as I reached for the knob. "Look at the dog."

The Lab was moving in circles, sniffing the floor. Suddenly she raised her head and with a joyous leap, bounded down the hall, disappearing into the dining room.

"She's on someone's trail," Julian said.

"Hey, maybe Bo's in the living room," Teena said. Her words were so hopeful I half believed she was right.

We hurried as fast as we could, sheltering our wildly waving candle flames, through the dining room and into the living room. Automatically I looked toward the chair where Bo had sat earlier, but it was empty.

"There's the dog," Julian said.

She was outside the closed door to the first room on the bedroom hallway, a room on the left, which should overlook the front of the house.

None of us spoke. We moved a step at a time through the archway, into the hallway to stand by the dog. She looked up at us and wagged her tail. Teena stroked the dog's head.

Julian opened the door slowly, pushing it inward, and I held my candle high, letting the light shine as far as possible into the room.

We were too frightened to cry out, too terrified to move. There, close to the door, stood the thronelike chair Teena and I had seen in the black room earlier. Across the ornately carved arms lay a sword, and resting on the sword, eyes closed, was Bo Baxter's head.

[TEN]

TEENA SAGGED against me, and Julian made a retching noise. The scene was such a shock it took me an agonizingly slow moment to react.

"It—it's an illusion!" I stammered. I shoved my candle at Julian, and when he grabbed it I hurried to the chair. "Look! There's a mirror! See—here, where it reflects the seat of the chair!"

I pulled at a small footstool that was wedged between Bo's rump and the calves of his legs. He was on his knees, with his head thrust through the opening in the back of the chair, the weight of his chest against a slanted mirror that stretched between the sword and the back of the chair seat. To anyone facing the chair the mirror reflected the same fabric as the back of the chair, giving the illusion of space between the sword and the seat. Bo's arms were tied, and the rope held his shoulders to the sides of the chair back.

"Julian! I need your knife!" I cried.

The knife was sharp, and fortunately the ropes were thin. It took Julian only a few moments to cut through them.

As Bo began to slide back I held his shoulders. Julian supported Bo's chin. The Lab wiggled between us, trying to lick Bo's face.

"Hold the dog!" I yelled to Teena, and she grabbed the Lab's collar, dragging her away. Julian and I carefully pulled Bo away from the chair and lowered him until he lay stretched out on the floor.

He groaned, and Teena shouted, "He's not dead!"

"Of course not," I said. "His breathing is a lot more regular than mine is." I felt his pulse and it seemed steady.

Julian knelt and pulled Bo's eyelids open. "His eyes look all right," he said. He felt around Bo's head and added, "He'll probably have a headache when he wakes up. I think he was hit on the back of the head."

Teena, who was still in the doorway, kept her eyes on the hall. "That was a horrible thing to do," she said. "I feel kind of sick to my stomach."

I glanced around the room. It was a simple bedroom with draperies and a bedspread that matched, a flowered pattern with a splash of giant purplish blossoms that crowded and cluttered the room. "Should we put Bo on the bed?" I asked.

"No," Julian said. He rubbed Bo's hands and Bo groaned again, his eyes fluttering open and shut like the wings of a lazy moth.

"Can we get him back to the kitchen?" Teena said. "I want to get out of here." She struggled with the dog, who began to whine and try to back out of the hallway.

I joined Teena at the door. From the light of our candles I could see the row of closed doors, with only that last one standing open.

"I don't like being so close to that room," Teena whispered to me. "And neither does the dog. Look how she's fussing to get out of here."

I nodded. I felt like a bug that was being lured closer and closer to a spider's strangling web.

"Dogs sense things," Teena said. "Something in that back room is scaring this dog."

"Julian," I said, "do you think we could manage to carry Bo?"

"We won't have to," Julian said. He tucked an arm under Bo's shoulders and helped him to a sitting position. "Do you think you can get up and walk, Bo?"

Bo rubbed the back of his head and stared at Julian. "What are we doing here?" he asked.

"Someone hit you and knocked you out," Julian said. "Do you remember what happened?"

Bo scrunched his eyelids closed and seemed to strain for the right memories. Finally he opened his eyes. "I was looking for the dog," he said. "I think I was in the living room. Or maybe—maybe it was the hallway. I remember wondering if the dog had gone into that last room. It was the only one with an open door." He looked bewildered. "Was that when someone hit me?"

"We don't know," Julian said.

"Where's—?" Bo twisted toward the doorway. He spotted the Lab and his eyes lit up. "Good! She's all right." He looked so relieved that Teena let go of the dog's collar and put her hands on her hips.

"The dog?" she said. "You're worried about the dog and not about Julian and Lisa and me?"

The dog bounded to Bo, this time licking his face without interference. Bo rubbed the dog's back, murmuring against her coat.

"Hah!" Teena exploded, but I put my hand on her arm.

"Teena, he was afraid something had hurt the dog. He knew we were all right."

"Hey, Bo," Teena ordered, ignoring what I had said. "Get your butt off that floor. We want to get out of this hallway."

I hurried to help Julian pull Bo to his feet. For a few moments Bo leaned against us. Then he steadied himself and straightened. "I'm okay," he said.

"Can you walk?"

"Sure." He winced. "I've just got one hell of a king-sized headache."

"I've got aspirin in my case in the kitchen,"

Teena said. "Let's get back there and fix you up."

The dog didn't want to go back in the hallway, but as soon, as Teena tugged her out of the bedroom she pulled away and dashed into the living room. From then on we made a strange procession, holding our candles high and walking slowly before and behind Bo as though he were royalty and we were his protecting minions. The Labrador stuck to Bo's side as though she were the most devoted slave of all.

As we approached the kitchen, gusts of damp air nearly extinguished our candle flames. We cupped our hands around them while we squeezed through the doorway.

"What happened here?" Teena said.

We stared at the back door, which was hanging open, swinging creakily on broken hinges. The chair that had propped the door closed was gone. Rainwater had sloshed across the floor, and the chairs and table were damp with spray. The dog shook herself as though she, too, were wet, and sat behind Bo's legs.

There was something in the far chair. I held up my candle and moved forward for a better look. Teena cried out before I did. In the chair—the one I had been sitting in—was what looked like a headless body. My sweater, which I'd last seen in a damp lump by the front door, was stuffed and propped in the chair, arms balanced on the table.

I walked closer to it. I could see the wadded newspapers under it and the mashed newsprint that was carefully tucked down inside the neck and arms of the sweater.

"What kind of creepy magic is that supposed to be?" Teena asked.

"It's not magic," I said. "I don't know what it means."

"It's a pretty strong message that we're not supposed to stay in the kitchen," Julian said.

"Someone wants us out of the house," Teena murmured, "but where can we go?"

"We don't have to do what that person wants us to do," Julian told her.

"Yeah? Keep the thought," Teena said.

I took a second look at the bare tabletop. "Someone's taken the scrapbook and the clippings."

Teena marched to the sink, put down her candle, which immediately blew out, and rinsed out a glass. "Good riddance," she said. "Before we do anything I'm going to see that Bo gets those aspirin." She filled the glass halfway with water and took it to Bo. Then she bent over and fumbled through her case until she found the aspirin bottle. She shook out two aspirin in her hand and held them up to Bo.

Obediently, without a word, Bo swallowed the aspirin and water, his Adam's apple bobbing up and down as he gulped. He wiped his mouth on his arm. "Thanks," he said to Teena.

Teena got to her feet. "What do we do now?"

"Get your candle," I said. "We'll have to find some other room where we can stay."

She brought the candle and held it out to mine. Sheltering it carefully, we managed to light it against the breeze from the open back door.

"Like where?" Teena asked.

Another door stood open as though it were beckoning us—the door to the black room. I felt as though someone invisible were standing there watching us, willing us to come in that direction. I couldn't see the person, but my feelings were strong. Black on black. Invisible. *Who are you? What do you want of us?*

"Come."

I jumped as the voice seemed to come from a spot next to my right ear. Was the word in my mind, or I had really heard it? The others had moved together and were busy lighting the other candles. Obviously they hadn't heard anything. Maybe the whisper had been my imagination. I shook myself as though I could toss the echoes of the word from my head.

As I stared at the doorway, Teena hissed in my ear, "Not on your life, Lisa! I know what you're thinking, and we're not going in that magic room!"

"How about the room with the bathroom across the hall?" Julian asked.

"Fine with me," Teena said, and she took a step toward me.

Julian glanced at the newspaper-stuffed sweater. "Do you want me to get your sweater, Lisa?"

"I don't even want to touch it!" I answered.

"Let's go!" Teena nudged me toward the hallway.

"Wait a minute," I told them. "Let's take our cases with us."

"We don't need the cases. I can just take the aspirin bottle," Teena said.

"No," I said. *Black on black.* "I have an idea. Take the cases. If we're bothered again we may need them."

Julian, Teena, and I bent down to pick up the cases. Bo turned to follow us out of the room as though he still weren't quite with it. But he walked a little faster, a little more steadily, as we crossed the hall and entered the empty room.

Julian was the last one inside, so he shut the door. "How about that!" he said. "A real lock!"

It was the little twisting kind below the doorknob, and as Julian turned it with a satisfying click, both Teena and I sighed with relief.

"I like that sound," Teena said. She laughed, but the tone was as dry as ancient dust.

Bo leaned against the wall, his feet flat on the floor, and his arms and head resting on his knees. The Lab curled up near him, put her head on her paws, and closed her eyes.

Teena sat beside Bo. "Is the aspirin helping any?"

"Yeah." Bo's voice was muffled. "It's helped a lot."

"Why don't you lie down? You can use my lap as a pillow if you want to."

Bo raised his head and looked at her. "Thanks, Teena," he said. "I'd like that." He scooted down and laid his head on her thighs. Like a mother with a napping child, she stroked his hair back from his forehead.

I put my case with the others and moved to the far wall, under the window. I wanted to be able to keep my eyes on that door. Julian sat beside me, close to me. I could feel the warmth of his body against my hip and shoulder, and I leaned against him.

Without a word Julian took my hand. I liked the feel of his long, slender fingers. They were strong and supple and reminded me of the hands in an El Greco painting.

I wished I could share my feelings with Julian, but how could I express my emotions in words? It would be like catching fistfuls of smoke, of wrapping arms around fog. These feelings were strangers to me, and I mistrusted them enough to keep them to myself. Was it comfort that I wanted, or was it more? Was I clinging to Julian because of love? Of fear? I had no perspective.

Forget perspective. My inner self, snugly curled like a purring cat against the warmth and fragrance of Julian's body, wanted nothing more than this moment. I began to relax.

Julian's voice was low, so only I could hear it. "When I met you at school I was afraid of you."

I looked up at him, my cheek brushing his. "Why? What's so frightening about me?"

He smiled. "I guess the word I mean is 'defensive.' I was sure you'd turn me down if I asked you for a date."

"I wouldn't," I told him. "I didn't know you were interested in dating me."

"You couldn't have guessed how I felt."

"No. I couldn't." I tried to remember Julian in class, our work together on the mime skit, our rehearsals. At the time I really didn't think about Julian at all—or Teena—or Bo. Who were those other people who had gone to the speech tournament together? They were characters in a play, another world away. They seemed to have nothing to do with the four of us in this room who were waiting for what would come next.

[ELEVEN]

"**B**O'S WATCH is gone," Teena said loudly. "I wonder what time it is."

"It's still dark," Julian said. "It's some time during the early morning hours, I guess."

"I don't like not knowing," Teena said. "It makes me feel like I'm floating in space. I want a time to hang on to."

I would have liked to float in space for a little while, anchored only to Julian, but Teena added, "We ought to talk about what's going on. We don't have a plan, an idea of who's in the house with us, nothing."

Bo struggled to a sitting position, rolling his shoulders back and forth, stretching his neck in and out like a rooster before it preens its feathers. "There's not much to talk about, is there?" he asked. "We can just stay here until it's light, then beat it out of this place."

"So far," I told him, "the person in here with us has dealt all the cards. We've done the best we can, but I think Teena's right. I think we should try to figure out who is in this house."

"It's the old lady, isn't it?" Bo asked.

"No little old lady was strong enough to get you in that chair," Julian said.

"What chair?" Bo asked. "I don't remember any chair."

So I described the head-on-a-sword trick. He looked sick to his stomach and gulped loudly. "What's all this stuff about heads?"

I gasped, and Julian turned to stare at me. "What are you thinking, Lisa?"

"The head on the pillow, the illusion with Bo, my headless sweater— It adds up. It's got to mean something."

"What?" Teena asked.

I was so frustrated not having the answer that I cried out, "I don't know!"

Julian squeezed my hand. "It's okay. Let's think about who this person is if it's not Mrs.

Gracie Ella. We're pretty sure it must be a man—someone fairly strong, because Bo's big and heavy."

"Everyone think," I said. "Let's just keep quiet for a few moments and go over everything anyone has done or said since we got to this house. Something is going to add up and make sense."

I closed my eyes, because it was easier to visualize, to remember. Black Beard inviting us inside, and the woman with him. What had she said? "What party?" No. Something else. Something about making another deal with hitchhikers. That was it!

"We think they brought a hitchhiker here," I said aloud.

"Who?" Bo asked.

"Black Beard and the woman," I said. "Remember when she asked him if he'd made another deal with hitchhikers? So we guessed they had been paid to bring someone to this house."

Julian nodded. "And they came back to bring him his jacket."

"But they couldn't find him here," Teena said. "Black Beard said the hitchhiker had left."

"He may have hidden from them. I don't think they'd had time to really look for him." Julian rubbed a finger on his chin as he thought.

"The television set had been turned on so loudly no one could hear what was going on," I said. "Why would the hitchhiker have done that?"

We all stared at each other. We were thinking the same thing. Teena whispered, "So no one would hear anything but the loud television if they came by." She shuddered.

"I think the hitchhiker is still in this house," I said.

"I'll give you that much," Teena said. "But who's this mean person supposed to be?"

"Harry Polowski," I said. "The Great Chamberlain." I explained to the others, "We found out his real name."

"But he's dead!" Teena said.

"Is he?"

"The newspaper clipping you read to me said he died in that theater fire."

"Teena," I said, "you're the one who asked me how they identified the body after it had been burned. What if the stagehand who was

on the critical list had really been Chamberlain, and it was the stagehand who was killed?"

"You're saying no one discovered this?" Julian asked. "That the Great Chamberlain's wife
got the insurance money with no problems?"

"That could have happened," I said, "if the
so-called stagehand was in no shape to speak
up about who he really was. A badly burned
person can be out of things for a long time.
And the stagehand who died could have been
one of those drifters no one knows, someone
with no family."

"But wouldn't Chamberlain say something
to the police when he began to recover?"

"Mrs. Whitt did say that the Great Chamberlain was a devil," Teena said. "Maybe he
found out what happened and decided he
wanted that insurance money, too."

"He'd have to go looking for his wife," Bo
said.

"Maybe he did," I said.

"How could she get mixed up about her
own husband and not identify him?" Teena
asked.

"Maybe she knew who he was, but liked
living with the money more than with him."

"You think that's what she did?"

"It might be why it took him two years to find her."

"Y'all sound so positive," Bo complained.

"It's because we're sure of one thing," I said. "Whoever is in this house with us is a magician. And he knows enough about the equipment here to find it and use it."

"Like the tapping hand." Julian's eyes narrowed.

"It has to be the Great Chamberlain," I said.

"One question," Teena said. "Where's Mrs. Gracie Ella?"

"It might help us if we just had more information," I said.

Bo twisted and tugged at something in his back hip pocket. "Maybe those letters will tell us something."

"I forgot the letters!"

"So did I. I just stuck them in my pocket because your arms were full."

He tossed me the letters, and I quickly tore off the string that held them together. The handwriting on the envelopes was the same.

"Some of these are addressed to Gracie Porter and some to Gladys Polowski. The ones to Gladys have P.O. box numbers." I stopped to explain what we found to Bo and Julian. "All these letters are postmarked in New Jersey. "They're from the same woman, Agnes Stanley," I added.

"Don't bother about the postmarks," Teena said. "What's in the letters?"

I held some of them out. "Let's all read some. If you come across anything that might tell us more about these people, you can read it aloud to the rest of us."

Teena scrambled across the floor, but Bo slumped against the wall and closed his eyes. "I'll pass," he said. "My head still hurts."

Julian, Teena, and I began to read. The letters seemed to be from someone close to Gracie Ella—or Gladys. "Gotta be her sister," Teena suddenly said. "She's writing here about something their mother said."

We read a while longer until Julian held up a hand. "Listen to this." He read, "'You told them that Harry was the one who died in the fire, but I get the feeling that you aren't that sure now. I'm worried, Gladys. You said the doctors expected that other man to die, but did you find out if he did? Did he ever regain consciousness? What if the insurance company gets after you for taking that money? And if Harry's the one who was on the critical list instead of the man they thought was the stagehand, and he recovers, he'll find you. You know he will.'"

Teena looked over his shoulder. "What's the date on your letter? Yeah, it's a lot later than this one. Wait till you hear what she's got in this. 'What you write about Harry scares me, Gladys. I think he's crazy and dangerous, and you ought to get away from him as fast as you can. I know what you mean about being afraid to be on your own, but lots of women have been in the spot you're in now, and they've managed to get away. You can't keep taking that abuse. The worst part of all—and I keep having nightmares about it—is that Harry might someday try to kill you. Right now he's like a cat with a mouse. He's always been like that. But remember that sooner or later the cat gets tired of playing with the mouse. Come stay with me, if you want. Harry knows where I live, but at least you'll have a home with me for a while, and that's better than not knowing where to go or what to do.'"

I picked up a letter from the pile I'd been reading. Now it made sense. "Listen to this one. She wrote it a little over two months ago. 'It's happened again. Someone has been phoning in the middle of the night and hanging up without saying a word. And when I opened my car door yesterday morning there was a dead cat lying on the front seat! Made me sick to my stomach! I think it could be some boys who live at the end of the block doing this to me, but I don't know why they'd pick on me for this awful game. Last week, after I found that tarantula in a jar on my nightstand, I went to see the boys' mother, but she denied that they'd done it. I just wish whoever is responsible would stop. This cat-and-mouse kind of thing is making me so nervous I can't stand it.'"

"Cat and mouse," Julian repeated, as I dropped the letter on my lap. "Just what she wrote earlier about Harry."

"Agnes Stanley died just a month ago," I said.

"Maybe it was a heart attack or something like that," Teena said.

"Maybe Harry killed her."

"That Mrs. Whitt didn't say Gracie Ella's sister was murdered." Teena scowled at me.

"Maybe no one knew it was a murder," Bo said. "There are ways of—"

"Shut up!" Teena yelled.

Bo just shrugged and turned to Julian. "Do you think she told him how to find her sister?"

"I don't think she would have done that," I said, "but Gracie Ella probably suspected what happened, and that's why she got rid of the trailer and moved the magic props inside."

"Why would she want to keep the magic props?" Bo asked.

I shrugged. "Mrs. Whitt wondered that, too. She said she seemed afraid to get rid of them."

"Harry must have had an awful hold on her," Teena murmured.

"There's a possibility," Julian said, "that Harry might have found Gracie Ella's address written down somewhere in her sister's house."

Teena threw her letter on the floor. "I don't

think reading these letters helped! I'm more scared than I was before!"

"Do y'all think the both of them are here in this house?" Bo asked.

For some reason they all looked at me. I thought about the strange things that had been happening to us, and my mind traveled into that dark hallway in which the only open door had been to the last room. My answer came out slowly. "Yes."

Teena shuddered. "I don't like the way you said that. I know what you're going to say, and I don't want to hear it!" She clapped her hands over her ears.

"What's she talking about?" Bo frowned at me.

Julian answered him. "I think we're all pretty sure that Mrs. Gracie Ella is dead."

"Oh," Bo said. "Yeah. I guess it figures. In that back room, huh?"

Julian nodded. "Whoever is in this house keeps trying to drive us out of whatever room we're in. At first I thought someone was just trying to frighten us into leaving the house. But now I wonder if he's trying to get us into that back room."

"Why?"

This time I answered. "Maybe he wants to show us what he's done."

Teena dropped her hands to her lap and clenched them tightly. Her eyes were scrunched up. "Or kill us there, too," she said. "The cat who finally gets tired of playing with the mice. What are we going to do?"

I held up a hand to silence her. My eyes were on the doorknob as it slowly, silently twisted back and forth. Someone was trying to get in the room!

We waited, motionless, staring at the doorknob. I gripped Julian's hand so tightly that my fingers were stiff and numb.

But just as suddenly as it had begun, the twisting stopped.

"Come." The whisper was clear, and it seemed to come from inside the room.

Bo's face looked like bleached cotton. His mouth worked as he stammered, "It's right here in the room with us!"

I swallowed a couple of times, and it was hard to get the words out. "He's a ventriloquist. Remember?"

"He's trying to get to us," Teena whimpered.

"We'll just stay put," Bo said. "There's no way we'll open the door."

"That's what we thought we could do in the kitchen," she said.

"Teena," I said, my voice as low as I could make it, "do you have an extra pair of tights with you? Black ones?"

"They've got a run in one leg," she said.

"That's okay. I've got a pair, too, and I've got an idea."

"What do my extra tights have to do with it?"

"Black on black," I said.

Julian's eyes widened, and he nodded. "Like our magician friend."

"He's not *my* friend!" Teena said.

"That's why we haven't been able to see him," I told them. "I think he's covered with black. It's an old stage trick. Black against black is practically invisible. If we wear our black tights and turtleneck shirts and can fix some head coverings and mittens from Teena's extra tights and an extra pair I brought along, we can try to beat him at his own game."

"Wait a minute," Teena said. She held up her candle. "He'd see us carrying these."

"We can put the candles at one end of the room."

"What room?"

"Black against black," I said.

Teena scrambled to her feet. The dog woke up and jumped on her, eager for action after her nap. Teena tried to push the dog away as she said, "Not in that magic room! No way! You're not going to get me in there, Lisa! Not on your life!"

"It may mean our lives," Julian said so quietly that Teena calmed down and stared at him. "I think we should do what Lisa suggests."

"Anyone have scissors or thread?" I asked.

"I've got fingernail scissors," Teena said.

"My mom put a package of safety pins in with my stuff," Bo said. "Will that help?"

"Sure," I said. "Julian, you and Bo go in the bathroom and get into your shirts and tights. Teena and I will see what we can make for head and hand coverings."

"I feel dumb in that stuff," Bo grumbled, but he picked up his case, followed Julian into the bathroom, and shut the door.

I pulled my case open and held up the tights. Teena just watched me. "Well," I said. "Where are your extra tights? And I need your fingernail scissors."

She leaned back against the wall, looking down at me. "I don't know if I like your being in charge," she said. "I have a feeling that you think like that magician."

"Maybe that's good," I said. "It might make it easier to figure out what he wants from us."

"But there's no telling what you're going to get us into."

"Get us *out* of," I said. "The object is to get us out of this house. Right?"

"But that black room with the magic stuff—"

She left the sentence unfinished. I stood and faced her. "Teena, that room may be a help to us. We may have to fight his magic with magic of our own."

"Will you know how to do that?"

"All I can do is try. But we've all got to work together."

Her antagonism slid away so quickly it left her face as soft and vulnerable as a small child's. "I want to go home," she said.

"So do I."

She reached out and gave me a quick, tight hug, then backed off as though she were embarrassed. "I'll give you my stuff," she said, and bent down to open her case.

I knelt beside her. "Look. We can make mittens from the feet in these things. Two pairs from the feet, and I'll cut the extra pair and the other parts we need from the legs. We'll make them just long enough to tuck in your sleeves and Julian's and Bo's."

Her glance was sharp. "What about you?"

"I don't think I'm going to need them," I said. "I'm the magician. Remember?"

We got to work; and as soon as Bo and Julian joined us, dressed in their turtlenecks, tights, black socks, and ballet shoes, we tried the mittens on them. Using Bo's safety pins to close the tops, we cut sections from the legs to fit over their heads.

"That looks scary!" Teena shuddered. "They look like stocking bandits, only worse."

"They don't frighten the dog," I said. She had jumped on Bo and was trying to lick his hands.

"Can you see through the fabric?" I asked.

"Enough," Julian said. "I can make out the shapes of things."

"It's okay," Bo said. "But I'd see more if you could cut slits for our eyes."

"You'd be surprised how the whites of your eyes would stand out," I told him. "If you can manage like this, it's better."

"Do we keep them on?" Bo asked.

"No," I said. "In fact, I don't want the Great Chamberlain to know what we've done. Put your clothes on over the black outfits, and stuff the head coverings and mittens in your pockets."

"How about you and Teena?" Julian asked.

"We'll put our stuff on now," I said, and I picked up my case and headed for the bathroom, Teena right behind me.

We didn't talk. There wasn't much left to say. We just got dressed as quickly as we could and went back into the bedroom. Julian and Bo were seated against the window wall. Teena and I joined them.

"I hope we don't have to go out of this room," Teena said.

"Y'all aren't the only ones," Bo added.

We were silent again. I rested my head against the wall and closed my eyes. Maybe the others felt as I did—almost too tired to be frightened. Or maybe fear wove itself into a smothering blanket, blotting out emotions until there was nothing left but a hollow, blank mind.

The sudden pounding at the other end of the house was so loud that we all started. The dog jumped up, alert, ears cocked.

"What—?" Teena said.

"The front door!" Bo said, his words tumbling over hers.

"It's someone outside the door!" Julian said.

A deep voice began shouting, "Open up! It's the police!"

"Thank God!" Teena yelled.

We scrambled to our feet, grabbing up our candles, bouncing off each other, and tripping over the dog as we raced to the door. Julian turned the lock and threw the door open. We rushed into the hall.

[TWELVE]

I T'S IMPOSSIBLE to run with a candle and not have the flame blow out. But when the flame I had so carefully sheltered disappeared in a puff, like a magician's assistant, I wasn't disturbed. The police were here. We'd be out of this house in a few moments.

Julian's candle was the only one still lit by the time we reached the front door. He held it out so that Bo could find the dead bolt and pull it back.

"Hurry!" Teena cried out.

It seemed as though time had stopped and Bo was moving in slow motion, but I knew that only a few seconds had passed before he flung the door wide.

No one was there.

Bo ran out on the small porch and down the steps. He turned to stare at us, arms held wide, shoulders lumped, the drizzle of tag-end rain pelting his face. "There wasn't any police car here," he said.

Teena took a step onto the porch as though she had to see for herself. "But we heard them pounding on the door. Someone yelled that it was the police."

"I'm afraid we were tricked," Julian said.

I groaned. "We should have known. We aren't within city limits. It wouldn't have been the police. Mrs. Whitt said she was going to call the sheriff."

"The crazy magician," Teena whispered. "Why is he doing this?"

No one had an answer. Without a word we watched the Lab as she ran out to join Bo. She dashed down to the drive, where the water covered her paws, running and splashing as though we were all playing a marvelous game.

Bo climbed the steps slowly until he was under the protective overhang. "It's not raining so hard as it was," he said. "Y'all notice that the water's going down?"

Pockmarks shimmered and flickered across the flat expanse of rain-speckled earth. It was like a giant pot of dark broth being peppered and salted. I could barely make out the road far beyond the wide expanse of lawn. There was no moon, only the glitter of the rain; and the darkness sucked in the outlines and shapes of everything it touched.

"Maybe we can wade through it," Teena suggested. "We could just keep walking down the road until we came to the next house."

The Labrador suddenly stopped bouncing, and leaped backward. She kept her eyes on a spot in the water. We could see a very slight rippling movement.

"Snake," Bo said. "There's bound to be snakes in the water this time of year. It's when they come out of hibernation, they'll go after anything that moves."

"Ugh!" Teena took a step back into the house. "It didn't get the dog, did it?"

"Naw," Bo said. "She'd be letting us know if she got bit." He whistled to the dog and slapped his leg, but the dog had seen or heard something. She raised her head and looked toward the road.

In the distance we could see a pair of lights wavering toward us.

"A car!" Julian said.

"A pickup truck," Bo corrected. "Those lights are too high to be a car."

"He's going fast," Teena said as the lights grew larger.

"Yell at him!" Julian said. He pushed forward so quickly that the flame on his candle blew out.

Teena jumped up and down, shouting and screaming. Bo, Julian, and I yelled, too. But the driver didn't see us, and with his windows rolled up tightly against the rain, he apparently didn't hear us either. His speed didn't lessen as his pickup truck went by, centering a double wall of water that swamped the sides of the road with waves.

"I can't believe it! He didn't hear us!" Teena's face was wet with tears.

The Lab bounded up on the porch, rubbing between our legs, trying unsuccessfully to find a place to shake off the drops of water that glittered against her sleek coat.

There wasn't room for all of us on that

little porch. I was wedged between Julian and the door frame, the dark living room to my back. "Bo," I said. "I hope you still have those matches in your pocket." As he fished for them and pulled them out I added, "We'll have to go back inside."

None of us took a step until our candles were lit, even though Bo struck most of the matches, trying to keep them alive in the cool wind. Finally, reluctantly, we went back into the living room. Julian closed the door as carefully and silently as though it were the lid of a carton of eggs. The Labrador, unaware of anything but her own comfort, shook herself vigorously, splattering us all.

"Please," Teena said. "Can we go back to the room we were in?"

Before any of us could answer her we heard a metallic, hammering sound in that direction, and Julian said, "It won't do any good. I have an idea that we just heard the lock on that door being broken."

The dog had stiffened, her head high, ears pointed. For only an instant she hesitated, then leaped toward the source of the sounds.

"Grab her!" Bo yelled. He leaped, but the dog was too quick for him, and she slid from his grasp as easily as a wet minnow.

He stumbled against Julian and me, and all of us nearly fell. The four of us stood, without talking or moving, waiting for something. I don't know what.

And it came.

There was a thud and a yelp. And silence.

"He hurt the dog!" Bo's face twisted in pain, as though he had felt it. "What kind of a bastard would hurt a dog!" His shoulders hunched forward, and he looked the way he did when he was going to charge down the football field.

"No!" Teena and I both yelled, and we grabbed him. Julian got in front of Bo and clutched his chin, pulling it upward. It took the three of us to hang on to Bo.

"You're not going after that dog!" Julian shouted into Bo's face, their noses almost touching.

Maybe it was the strength in Julian's voice that made Bo listen to him. He stopped struggling. He took a couple of long breaths that must have reached his toes. Julian, Teena, and I just watched, waiting for what he might do next.

Finally he turned to face us, and he was angry. His feet apart, his shoulders down, he still looked ready to charge an opposing team. "Why didn't you let me go?"

"We didn't want you to get hurt," Teena said.

"It's just one of him against us," Bo said. "Why don't we rush him?"

"How are we going to rush someone we can't see?" Julian asked.

Bo thrust his chin out with such intensity that it quivered. He turned toward the direction from which the sound had come. "Get out here, you S.O.B.!" he yelled. "Get out and face us, you coward!"

I sucked in my breath, listening, wondering what the answer would be. But there was no answer.

"It's got to be light pretty soon." Teena's voice held a spill of tears. "Isn't it almost morning?"

Bo's right hand clasped his bare wrist. "I don't know," he said. The bravado had vanished, leaving only discouragement.

The thought didn't come in words. It wasn't even a feeling I could pinpoint. It was like a tug at my mind, a compulsion to move across that room toward the sideboard. So I did.

The light from my candle moved ahead of me to touch the photograph of the Great Chamberlain and Gracie Ella—the one I had carefully propped into position. It had been torn from top to bottom, and the top-hatted magician's shoulder rubbed only ragged edges.

"Look what he's done to his picture," I called to the others. "He must hate his wife."

The others joined me, and Julian bent his candlelight to the floor. "He must have thrown away the rest. Yes, here it is." He stooped and picked up another piece of the photograph.

"Her head's gone." Bo's voice was loud.

No one spoke until Teena groaned and clapped one hand over her mouth. She was staring with horrified eyes at a spot near the top of the arrangement of roses.

There, impaled on a dried stem, where a blossom had once been, was the rest of the picture—the shyly smiling face of Gladys Polowski.

"What do we do now?" Bo mumbled.

"I guess it's his move next." Julian seemed to be talking to himself.

"He's got all the moves," Teena said.

"Damn, I wish I had my rifle with me," Bo said.

"We haven't got anything to fight back with." Teena's voice had risen, becoming shrill.

I put an arm around her shoulder, holding her tightly. "Yes, we have," I said.

She squirmed, trying to move away from me. "What? Not your idea of black—"

I clapped one hand over her mouth, shaking her with the other. "Stop that!" I yelled.

She did stop, looking at me with such amazement that I took my hand away and said quietly, "Don't blab it, Teena. You've got more sense than that."

"I don't even know what you've got in mind," Teena told me.

I motioned toward the chairs we had first sat in when we came to this house. "Keep it down," I said. "We do have a chance it we meet him on his own ground."

The others followed me, but instead of sitting on the chairs, we crawled into a tight circle on the floor. I reached for Julian's hand and was thankful for the strength in his fingers, which were wrapped so comfortingly around mine.

"How are we going to do that?" Teena was scornful.

Bo put a hand on her shoulder. "Dammit, Teena! Will you listen to Lisa?"

"I'm tired of listening to what other people want me to do," she said. She glared at Bo. "How about you, big football hero? Aren't you sick of always doing what somebody else tells you to do? Like your daddy?"

"Come off it, Teena," Julian said. "It didn't take us long to figure out we're all in the same boat."

"That's right," I said slowly. "We're all illusionists."

"You're telling us we're all magicians? You're crazy," Teena said.

"I'm saying that we're all illusionists. We're pretending our lives. We're saying, 'Look right here, ladies and gentlemen, at this good young person doing just what my mother and father and brothers and sisters want me to do, being what they want me to be. I'm going to be fill-in-the-blank and make everyone proud of me and live happily ever after.' Only it's not for real.

"It's Julian saying for the rest of his life, 'Come right in, Mrs. Jones, and we'll find out what's causing that nasty cough.' And the person behind the doctor illusion is listening to the music and dancing in a world he never let happen."

I turned to Teena. "And you. If you're a judge, I'd hate to come before you, because that illusion who's sitting on the bench will be playing a bitter role as she thinks of the real Teena who wanted to explore, wanted to find her own way."

"How about Lisa?" Teena said. "Aren't you an illusion, too?"

"My illusion is back at school, getting stomach pains from the pressures of not measuring up," I said.

"I don't understand what you're talking about," Bo said. "We're wasting time with all this weird stuff about illusions. Just tell us what you've got in mind, Lisa, so we'll know what to do."

"That's simple, childlike trust," Teena said.

"I trust Lisa," Julian told her.

We all looked at Teena. She hesitated just a moment, then said, "We haven't much choice."

Julian put an arm around my shoulders. "We have choices," he said. "We can keep waiting to see what this magician will do next and try to survive, trick by trick, wondering which trick will be our last."

"Come on," Teena said, but she glanced behind her into the dark room.

"We didn't want to work on the mime skit together," Julian said. "We didn't want Bo's car to break down. But that's the way life is. We didn't get to choose our parents or the kind of homes we live in or even our own bodies, but we can control what we've got. We don't have to follow someone else's orders if we've got brains enough to think for ourselves."

Bo spoke up, his words filled with a self-wonder. "I know what you mean, Julian. It's like getting an elbow hard in the solar plexus. You get up and you keep playing."

"Julian, the doctor, saying all that?" Teena tried to look cocky and didn't make it.

"Maybe Julian, the dancer," he said. He looked at me and smiled. "I guess I never thought to tell my parents how much I wanted to be a dancer."

"If you decide to tell them, will they help you?" I asked.

"New York's full of people working their own way through the training they need," he said. "I'm not afraid of work." He held me more tightly and said, "New York's probably a good place for a magician to get started, too."

Teena let out a long sigh. "I have an idea, if anybody's interested."

"Of course we are," I told her. "What is it?"

"I think we should stay out of the black room." She raised both hands before any of us could answer and said, "I'm not finished. I'm saying that I don't think we need all sorts of hocus-pocus stuff that Lisa's got in mind. I think we just need to be an audience."

She paused, and Julian said, "Go on."

"Think about this guy, if he is the Great Chamberlain. He's been away from his business for a long time, spending at least the last couple of years recuperating and trying to find his wife to get even. Right?"

"That makes sense," Bo said.

"So what does a guy who's in show business like? An audience. Okay? Maybe that's why he's doing these things to scare us. He wants to show off his tricks."

I shook my head. "Just a little while ago you said you thought he might—"

She interrupted me, holding out her trembling hands as though trying to stop my words. "Don't say it. Don't even think it. I changed my mind."

Julian frowned. "He hurt Bo." He paused. "And the dog. That was more than just showing off."

"We don't know what happened to the dog," Teena said. "And there was no way the magician could have got Bo to stick his head in that chair without knocking him out."

"What are we supposed to do?" Bo asked. "Sit here and applaud?"

Teena didn't look sure of herself, but she answered, "That's kind of what I had in mind."

Julian turned to me. "What do you think, Lisa?"

"Do we have to do what Lisa thinks?" Teena shouted.

"Calm down," I said, sharing the desperation I saw in her eyes. "You might be right. We don't really know much about this guy. If anything, it will buy us some time."

Teena glanced toward the dark windows, opaque with rain. "If we can just hold out until morning—until someone comes—"

"Let's give it a try," I said. "What do you want us to do?"

"Let's sit down, facing the archway. We can applaud and ask him to put on a show for us."

"I don't think it's going to help," Julian said.

"Try it!" Teena urged, and I nodded.

"Let's do try it," I said to Julian.

"Why not?" Bo said.

"Tell us where to sit." Julian looked at Teena, and she pointed at a spot on the floor, not too far from the entrance to the hallway, but allowing room for a stage.

"Leave the candles on the sideboard," she said.

We sat close together, Teena and I in front of Bo and Julian. We waited for a few minutes, but nothing happened.

Teena suddenly called out, "We're ready for

the magician's act! Come on, Great Chamberlain!" In a low voice, meant just for us, she said, "Get with it! Applaud."

We did. Bo whistled, and Teena banged her feet on the floor. "Keep it up until he does something," she said.

My palms were beginning to sting when a silver cane suddenly caught the candlelight, glittering from the darkness in the hallway. We quieted, and I found it hard to breathe as an invisible magician pulled a row of scarves from the cane, sweeping them up and away until they became invisible, too.

There was a pause, and as though we had been prompted we all burst into applause again. The cane became a wild bouquet of flowers, and our applause grew more enthusiastic.

"I think it's working," Teena whispered to me.

A white top hat appeared, held by those black-on-black, invisible hands.

"Will he bring out a rabbit?" Teena murmured.

I half believed he would, since from childhood I was used to seeing the rabbit-in-the-hat trick; so it was as chilling as a shower suddenly turning cold to see him pull out and fling into the air crudely cut strings of paper dolls—the kind we made in kindergarten—all of them without their heads.

None of us applauded, and a deep chuckle came from the void.

Julian leaned forward, and his fingers found mine. I didn't know whether he was comforting me or needed comfort himself. I held his hand tightly, glad we could help each other.

"Maybe we shouldn't have started this," Teena whispered. "I'm really getting scared now!"

I felt the touch of his mind again. He wouldn't be satisfied with small tricks. No magician would. There were the disappearing balls, the coins, the quickly vanishing water-in-the-pitcher, all the standard warm-up tricks. But this magician would want more than that. I should have realized that if he were hungry for an audience, as Teena thought, he'd want to do his biggest and best. I had to stop the show! Now!

The water pitcher appeared, as though I had ordered it, and the hands poured water into a glass. The glass was raised to pour the water back into the pitcher, when I managed to get to my feet on shaky legs. I tugged my hand from Julian's grasp. "Thank you," I said loudly. "Good show. Good tricks. Thank you very much." I began to applaud.

"What are you doing, Lisa?" Bo asked.

Julian reached for my hand and was trying to pull me down when a flash of light nearly blinded me and a loud explosion hurt my ears. I dropped to my knees, tucking my head against Julian's shoulder.

For a few moments there was nothing but confusion. Teena had screamed. Or maybe it was me. Then something in my memory reacted.

"Flash powder!" I yelled. "Nearly every magician uses flash powder."

The powder had left a residue of smoke in the room, and we backed away, coughing. I bumped against Bo, clutched at Julian's arm, and reached out for Teena.

"Teena? Where's Teena?"

We stared at each other through the haze. I couldn't think. I guess I was waiting for someone to say, "Here she is. Everything's all right."

Instead, Teena screamed, and her scream came from another part of the house.

"The magic room!" I stammered. "It has to be! I should have known!"

Without even grabbing for a candle, I ran into the dreaded hallway and through the first door on the right. It was the quickest way. I stumbled into a spindly chair that had been pulled back from a small desk and flung it out of my way. I could hear the others running close behind me. I could see the candelabra resting on a pile of boxes, only two of its candles lighting the way into the black-walled storage room.

I stopped so suddenly that Bo charged into me, and I would have fallen if he hadn't grabbed my arms. He let out a string of profanity, and Julian took a step forward.

"Wait!" I told him.

Before us, close to the center of the room, was the traditional cabinet with slots on all sides—slots to hold the pile of swords that rested nearby. Locked in the cabinet, with only her head visible, was Teena.

[THIRTEEN]

"HELP ME," she whimpered.

The room was so dim it was hard to see beyond the cabinet, but a sword suddenly flashed upward. It entered the bottom slot on the right, moving across to the other side.

Teena cried out. "It just missed me!"

"We'll get you out of there," Bo said, but a small flash of powder exploded almost at his feet.

Another sword rose high, and a deep chuckle rolled from the blackness.

"Teena," I said, "pay attention to me. Do what I tell you. That cabinet is an old one. I've seen others like it."

The second sword slid into the cabinet on the other side. Teena screamed again.

"She's not hurt," I yelled at Bo and Julian. I tried to calm down, but I couldn't stop shaking. "Teena! In that trick the first sword is real. The others are only an illusion!"

"How could a sword be an illusion?" Bo muttered.

Frantically, angrily, I pushed him, calling to Teena, "Those are trick swords. There's a place to snap them apart as they come into the cabinet. Do it, Teena!"

I waited, holding my breath, but nothing happened. The room was silent. Even Teena, her eyes wide and terrified, didn't make a sound.

"Maybe I'm wrong, but I think he's backed off," I whispered to Julian, and he hurried forward, pulling out the swords. Bo rushed to join him, opening the latch on the cabinet.

They had to help Teena out. Her legs wobbled like those of a marionette with loose strings.

"I was wrong about him," she said, as we all tried to comfort her, and she began to cry.

"No! You were right. He needs an audience," I told her. I kept my voice low, wondering where the magician was hiding, sure he was somewhere in this room. I tried to make out the shapes of the boxes and cartons, and I could see a pair of traditional rectangular, narrow cabinets used for the act in which two assistants switch places. There was also a large wooden chest with a rope curled on top. I knew what that was for and guessed there'd be a padlock with it. That was all I needed.

"He's going to win, isn't he?" Teena said.

Bo patted her back. "I wish I had my rifle," he said.

"He's not going to win if we can outthink him," I told Teena. "We can try my plan. If it doesn't do anything else, at least it will delay things."

She raised her head from where it rested on Bo's shoulder. "Delay what?"

They all looked at me. "We saw the opening warm-up," I said. "He was moving into the more exciting acts. But there's always a grand climax. Magicians save the best for last."

"Do you know what it's going to be?" Julian's voice was low.

"Not exactly," I said. "But I know *where* he wants it to be."

"That back room at the end of the hall," he said, and I nodded.

"I'm going to challenge him," I said. "Magician to magician." Even as I spoke the words I wondered how I dared try it. He was a pro, and 'Shandra, the Wonder Girl' wasn't that wonderful.

"But he knows his own tricks," Julian said. "How will you be able to surprise him?"

"By doing them just a little differently," I said, adding, "with your help."

"Is this where the black outfits come in?" Bo asked.

"Yes," I said, "but not just yet." I pulled the others close to me, hoping that the Great Chamberlain was far enough away so that he wouldn't hear us. We had all kept our voices low, but I spoke even more softly as I explained.

"I'm going to put Bo and Julian into the matching cabinets," I said. "If they're as ancient as the rest of this equipment, I'm betting they have false sides and a bar up and down in front between two opening doors. Those sides have mirrors on the parts that are hidden when they're against the cabinets' walls. When you want to 'disappear' you release their small catches—which you should be able to feel—and swing the sides toward the center. They'll come to a point at the bar, and when the cabinet is open the mirrors reflect the interior sides of the cabinet, making it look as though the cabinet is empty. Do you understand that part?"

"Yes," Julian said.

"I guess so," Bo said, "but how does our disappearing do any good?"

"In the standard act, you'd not only disappear, but when the cabinets were opened the final time you'd have changed places. I'm counting on the Great Chamberlain to expect that, because we're not going to do it that way."

I looked around the room again, but there was no sign that he was near. The light from the pair of candles reached only so far, but in that ring of light I felt safe.

"It's too complicated to teach you the switching part," I said, "and we don't need it. I'll put you in the cabinets and close the doors.

Then I'll open them once again just to prove that you're still there. When I close them the next time, I want you to take off your shirts and jeans, so that you'll be dressed in black. Put on your hoods and mittens, and creep out the backs of the cabinets."

"They open in back?" Bo asked.

"Of course."

"All of this magic stuff is fake," Teena said.

"It has to be," I said. "You know it's all illusion. The trick is for the magician to make you think you see what you don't see. Or to keep you from seeing what he doesn't want you to see. And that's what we're going to do."

"How about me?" Teena said. She took a deep breath. "Tell me what to do, and I'll do it."

I looked at her. "Remember what I said about diversion? How a magician sometimes gets the audience's attention on one thing so they won't see something else he's doing?"

"Yes."

I just stared at her for a moment. I felt kind of sick. What if my idea didn't work? "Teena, you'll have to be the diversion. While he's watching what I'm doing with you, Bo and Julian can move around behind him."

"Take him by surprise," Julian said. He frowned as he thought, and I hoped it wasn't because he was afraid the plan would fail.

"You didn't tell me what I'd have to do," Teena said slowly.

"There's an old trick with a wooden chest," I told her. "You'll get in the chest, and I'll padlock it and tie it with a rope."

She closed her eyes for a moment. "Oh, Lisa, I couldn't do that. Not after—"

"It's okay," I said. "You'll be able to get right out. Those chest have sliding partitions at the back. Or some of them have doors that open in. All you have to do, once I close the lid, is pull off your shirt and jeans, so you'll be all in black, open the partition, and climb out the back. It will be a small opening, but you're small, too, so you shouldn't have any problem getting out. Then you can slip on your hood and mittens and crawl as far away from there as you can, so no one can see you."

"How will I find the way to open the back?"

"You'll just have to feel your way. When I'm at the cabinet I'll be able to tell if it's a sliding door or one that opens in. I'll do what I can to help you figure out how the door opens. That's the best I can do."

She was silent for a moment. "Could I try it out first?"

I looked at each of them in turn. They waited, trusting that I knew what I was doing. All I could do was hope I was right. "There's no way in the world to try it out," I said. "Magicians and their assistants practice for hours and hours to get each trick right, but we can't do that. We have to do it once and make it work the first time."

"I'm scared to death," Teena said. "What if I get in there and can't get out?"

"That magician may be smarter than Lisa is," Bo said. "What I mean is, he's been a magician for years, and Lisa's—well—an amateur. In football, there wouldn't be any contest between a pro and an amateur."

"I know," I said. "Believe me, I've thought about that. You're right, Bo. We don't have to do this."

"Yes, we do," Julian said. "It's a good plan, and I trust Lisa."

"I don't know if I trust Lisa so much," Teena said, "but I keep thinking about that room at the end of the hall. We've got to do something, and the idea I dreamed up sure fell apart."

"When do we do all this?" Bo asked.

We moved just slightly away from each other, our eyes straining as we searched the room. I was afraid our magician had left to plan something for which we wouldn't be prepared, but a slight sound on the other side of the room told me he had bumped into one of the boxes and was still nearby.

"Chamberlain the Great!" I called, my voice hoarse and cracking in spite of my determination. "I challenge you to a duel of magic!"

Another deep chuckle was the only answer. It made me angry, and the anger gave me courage. "Are you afraid I'll win?" I called.

The silence was that of an animal tensed and waiting to spring. I drew on all the bravery I could muster and said loudly, "Maybe you're afraid because your skills are old and rusty, like your equipment."

I heard him move closer, brushing against a box. Was he careless because I had made him angry? Maybe anger was a tool I could use.

"We saw your opening act," I said. "It wasn't that great. Let me show you *my* technique. Even using your magic tools I can mystify and astound you!"

The rasping whisper was so hollow and so chilling that for an instant I wondered if I could be dealing with someone from another world. "Challenge accepted," he said.

"Come on," I said, taking Julian's and Teena's hands and leading them to a spot near the cabinets. Bo followed closely. In a whisper I showed them how to place the cabinets, with the wooden chest in front and between them. Helping to move the equipment gave me a chance to get familiar with the pieces. They were just what I had hoped they'd be.

"Help me with this chest," I said to Teena. As we tugged it into place, our heads down, I whispered, "It's a panel. Push here, on this side. It should slide back."

Finally the equipment was where I wanted it to be. I stepped to a spot in front of the chest and addressed the darkness. Our only light came from the pair of candles in the candelabra near the door. Blackness dissolved into shadows with ragged, yellowed edges, touching the squared shapes of boxes and equipment and giving me a wavering, unreal light in which to perform. At least he couldn't see how much I was trembling.

I had no idea where Chamberlain would be, but I knew where an audience would be seated, and I pretended I was performing for an eager, receptive bunch of kids. One tiny thought nagged at me, urging me to turn and run in terror, but I clung to the magic I could do and the magic I could be. I began the act.

"Two of my assistants," I said, "will enter this pair of cabinets. If you look closely, you'll see that the cabinets are empty. We'll turn them around, like this, so that you can be sure they are simple wooden cabinets."

I rapped on the side of the one closest to me.

"Not only will my assistants disappear on command, they will exchange places, so that when I open the doors you will see that they have moved to opposite cabinets."

Bo got a puzzled look on his face. I could see Julian press one foot on the toe of Bo's shoe. I hoped Bo got Julian's message. He couldn't ruin this trick! Oh, please, no!

"In this first cabinet, I'll place one assistant," I said. I nudged Bo, and as he climbed in I closed the doors.

I walked with Julian to the second cabinet, a few feet away. "And in this cabinet, I'll place my second assistant."

As I closed the doors behind Julian I felt even more vulnerable, more terrified than before, as though Teena and I were alone with this invisible horror. Teena stood as though she were frozen, her eyes wide and unblinking. It was hard for me to find the words I needed.

"You'd like to see them again before they vanish?" I asked my invisible audience. "Very well. I'll prove to you that they're still here."

I opened Julian's door, and he formally nodded at the invisible audience. Julian would never know how glad I was to see him. In this strange, dark, hocus-pocus fantasy world, I had to prove his existence to myself as well.

After closing the doors, I walked to Bo's cabinet and opened it wide, holding my breath, hoping for the best. Bo shrugged, not knowing what was expected of him. He shifted from one foot to another and bent toward me. "Lisa," he whispered, "where—?"

Bo! You've got to do it right! I waved my left hand toward Julian's cabinet, calling, "You have seen the cabinet on your right, ladies and gentlemen! Will you knock on the walls, please, Julian, to prove you're still there."

As Julian responded, giving me the diversion I needed, I took Bo's fingers and pressed them against the catch that held one of the mirrors.

"Oh. Okay," Bo said.

I closed the doors on Bo. "You have seen the cabinet on your left. You know both cabinets contain my assistants. And now—now I will say a few magic words, and my assistants will disappear!"

Rapping on Julian's cabinet I shouted, "Abracadabra!" which was the only thing that came into my head. I might lose points with the Great Chamberlain for lacking imagination, but if the trick worked, it wouldn't matter.

I opened the doors to Julian's cabinet, and the empty-seeming space was so effective, Teena gasped. I shut the doors.

"And now for my other assistant," I said,

moving to Bo's cabinet. *Please, Bo, do it the way it's supposed to be done!* Repeating my magic word I threw open the doors of the cabinet. Thankfully, Bo was tucked behind the secret mirrors. The cabinet looked empty.

Closing the doors I said, "It will take a little time, ladies and gentlemen, for the magic transfer to work." I heard the low chuckle again, and it gave me hope that Chamberlain thought I'd really try the switch.

"So in the meantime," I said, "I'm going to put my third assistant into this chest in the middle of our stage. She will be locked inside the chest with a padlock, and this rope will be tied around the chest. She, too, will be made to disappear!"

I lifted the lid of the chest and took Teena's hand to help her climb inside. She was so frightened she was shaking, and she stumbled, clutching my hand, as she stepped over the high edge of the chest.

The padlock was stiff and a little rusty, but I held it high and said, "Will someone in the audience please come forward and examine this padlock and put it in place as I close the lid?"

I guess it was crazy to hope that Chamberlain would respond. Of course he didn't. I waited only a moment, then lowered the lid of the chest. It was like closing the lid of a coffin. Teena scrunched herself into a ball, arms clasping her knees, head tucked down. Her whimper was so soft that only I could hear it.

"Please, ladies and gentlemen, I need someone to testify that this is a genuine padlock and the chest will be securely fastened."

Again I waited, and this time I thought I heard Chamberlain move closer. I didn't really expect him to respond to my invitation to test the padlock, but I hoped to lure him closer to the candlelight, where he could be seen. Maybe it was my imagination, maybe just wishful thinking, but I was sure I saw a movement between two large boxes. There was a faint outline, tall and rounded and humped. If only Bo and Julian could see him, too!

"All right," I said, trying to sound strong and sure of myself, "if there are no volunteers, then you will have to take what I say and do on trust. I am locking this chest with the padlock." I moved around the chest with the rope, tying it loosely and with difficulty. I wished I weren't so clumsy, but there was no way I could get the rope under and over the chest without help. Tying it around the side would have to suffice.

Bo and Julian should be on their way out of the cabinets by now. I tried to be loud and distracting, in case they made any noise.

"Ladies and gentlemen, wonder of wonders, when I open this chest you will discover—" I was shouting. Would Chamberlain see through my attempts? It was just the two of us facing each other. He was no longer invisible. The rounded hood—which is what it seemed to be—had separated itself from the shadows, coming just a little closer to me.

From where I stood, giving my inane patter, I could see the back panel of the chest shake a little. Oh, no! It must be warped and stuck! Teena couldn't open it!

I don't know what I said to my audience of one as I tried to stall for time. I'm sure most of it didn't make sense.

"Wait, ladies and gentlemen," I announced, as the chest shook with Teena's efforts to get free. "I am almost ready to magically transfer my assistant from this chest, making her become invisible."

It was obvious we were in trouble, and Chamberlain broke into a grating, husky laugh. He had chosen his time, and it was now. He moved forward, step-by-step, and I could see the outline of his black hood as he came closer and closer to me.

My plan hadn't worked. Teena was trapped in that old chest, and I didn't know where Julian and Bo were! I had nothing left with which to fight. I was so frightened I was unable to move, to even lift my arms to try to protect myself. I screamed, and at the same time two black figures seemed to fly through the air. The hooded figure dropped and disappeared in a kicking, grabbing scramble of arms and legs.

I raced for the candelabra, and by the time I had brought it back, Bo was sitting on the magician and Julian was pulling the rope from the chest.

They tied him with it, and we turned him over and pulled back the hood. The man's face was badly scarred, his misshapen features twisted in anger. He spat at us, struggled against the rope, and shouted curses. When his eyes met mine, he suddenly became quiet; but I stepped backward, shaken by the hatred that shot toward me like a laser beam. "She sent for you, didn't she?" he said to me. A raspy noise rumbled from deep in his throat, a weird kind of laughter. "But you were too late. Too late."

A pounding came from inside the chest. "Teena!" I said. I pulled at the outside of the panel, but it didn't move. "She can't get out of the chest! And I haven't got a key for the padlock! Can you break it?"

"The panel will be easier," Julian said. He and I tugged and hammered at the sliding partition until it finally gave way, sticking and resisting as we forced it open.

Teena crawled out, stood up, and shouted, "Lisa! Your stupid idea! I could have been stuck in there forever! And it was horrible! You don't know how scared I was!"

Suddenly she saw Bo on the floor with Chamberlain. She looked from me to Julian and back again. "It worked!" she said.

"We don't know how much longer we'll be here," Julian said. "And we're pretty much shut off from everything if we stay in this room." He looked at Bo. "Do you think we can carry him into the living room?"

"Sure," Bo said. He grunted as he stood, staring down at Chamberlain. "We can grab him under his arms and drag him."

"Let's do it," Julian said.

Bo cocked his head as he looked at Julian. "You know, y'all are a lot stronger than you look. The way you handled that guy was real neat. And I've been watching you. You move good. Ever thought about trying out for a placekicker?"

"A what?"

Bo looked as though he couldn't believe Julian had asked the question. "Everybody knows what a placekicker does," he explained. "He's the guy who comes out just to kick the field goals or get that ball over on a conversion. Sometimes they're little guys, or skinny, but they can kick, and that's what made me think of you."

Julian smiled. "Thanks, but I don't think I'd really be interested."

"They make good money in pro ball."

Julian bent down to grab Chamberlain under his right arm. "I'll keep it in mind," he said.

We went back to the living room the way we had come. Chamberlain struggled as they dragged him, making it a lot harder. And he yelled threats. Some of them must have been at us, but it was hard to tell, because sometimes he seemed to be talking to his wife. I moved ahead to open the door wide, and Teena carried the candelabra. I shuddered as we entered the hallway, and I noticed that all of us carefully avoided looking in the direction of the open door at the end of the hall.

Julian and Bo dumped Chamberlain in the middle of the room. "I've got to find the dog," Bo said, as though he'd had nothing else on his mind all the time.

"Go ahead," Julian said. "I'll keep an eye on this guy."

We watched Bo go into the dining room. The others probably felt the way I did. I ached for Bo with the same pain I'd feel for a close friend who had lost something he loved.

Bo appeared, returning through the archway, carrying the Labrador across his arms, hugging it close to his chest. Even in the dimness I could see the tears spilling down Bo's cheeks.

I held tightly to Julian, my words coming out in a sob. "Oh, no!"

"It's okay," Bo said, and he grinned at us. "This old girl's alive. I'll take care of her. She's going to make it."

I found I'd been crying, too. And I wasn't the only one. As we hugged each other, I realized that all of our faces were damp.

Bo, cradling the Labrador, plopped on the floor next to Chamberlain, who glared at Bo in the same terrifying way he had glared at me. But it didn't seem to bother Bo. "I'm staying right here until the police come for you," he said to Chamberlain, and he began gently stroking the dog's neck.

"Hey!" Teena suddenly said. "Notice something? It's getting light!"

We rushed to the front door and threw it wide, eagerly opening it to the morning.

The trees, their new leaves glimmering and dripping, were stark against the silvered light. Water had soaked into the sodden ground, and the lawn was a scramble of twisted blades of grass and mud. Beyond the road a lone black grackle cawed stridently and flapped his way to the top of a telephone pole.

Teena sighed. "No one knows how good that looks to me!"

I laughed. "We do!"

"Yeah," she said and giggled. "I guess we all do."

Julian put an arm around me. "The speech tournament seems a hundred years ago. I don't even feel like the same person."

"You aren't," I said. "I don't think any of us is the same. After what we went through we couldn't be." Maybe I had wondered if my feelings for Julian had been so tied in to my fear that they were an illusion, too. I had wanted someone to cling to. I recognized this. But here, in the safety of morning, with the closeness of his body warming mine, I knew my feelings were real. It was a weird time and place in which to be happy, but I was.

"I know for sure I'll never be so afraid again," Teena said. "Maybe I'll never be afraid of anything—ever."

"Don't count on it," I said.

"Maybe I'll even be brave enough to do

some of that exploring you talked about, Lisa. I've got a year before I graduate. That will give me time to think about what I want to do."

"I've already been thinking," I said. "I might even end up being a magician."

"You need a lot of practice," she said. "Your act was really bad."

We laughed, and I hugged Julian. "Okay," I said, "I admit it, but at least right now I feel good about myself, and that's an improvement."

"How about you, Bo?" Julian said. With one arm around me he walked back into the living room. Teena came with us.

Bo looked up. "How about what?"

"We're being introspective," Julian said. "Did this do anything to change your outlook on life?"

"Y'all waste a lot of time talking about nothing," Bo said. "What we should be thinking about is getting in touch with the sheriff."

When the phone rang—a loud, jangling intrusion—we all started. Teena let out a yelp, but she was the first to dash back into the living room to answer it.

"Yes, Mrs. Whitt, we're still here," she said. "No. We didn't know the phones were back in order." She listened for a while, nodding. Finally she broke in. "Yes. What the sheriff told you was right. We thought—we hoped Sam would call him. Do you think they'll get here soon?"

Mrs. Whitt's answer was brief, because Teena said, "Good. Thanks for calling." She hung up the receiver. "I don't think we'll have to wait very long."

Julian took the phone. "We'll make a call ourselves. It might be better that way."

"And we can all call home," Bo said. "We'll probably have to go in with the sheriff, and I'd kind of like to have my daddy on hand."

"I hope they don't make us go in that back room," Teena said. "I don't want to know what's in there. I haven't even let myself think about it."

Don't you know? I thought, and shuddered. *But I know. With all his strange, twisted clues the Great Chamberlain had told us.*

As though she were tuning into my thoughts, Teena leaned on the sideboard and picked up the little guillotine that stood near her hand. "Lisa," she said, "you told us this was part of a set. Where is the big one?"

Have you read these
Joan Lowery Nixon books?

The Kidnapping of Christina Lattimore

WINNER OF THE EDGAR ALLAN POE AWARD
FOR BEST YOUNG ADULT MYSTERY

Christina is accused of masterminding
her *own* kidnapping.

The Séance

WINNER OF THE EDGAR ALLAN POE AWARD
FOR BEST YOUNG ADULT MYSTERY

The séance starts as a game, but it leads to
murder and terror for a small Texas town.